PERFECT NIGHT

TERRI E. LAINE

Perfect NIGHT

MASON CREEK

USA TODAY BESTSELLING AUTHOR
TERRI E. LAINE

Sarah Paige @ The Book Cover Boutique - cover design
Lindee Robinson Photography for couple photo

ONE

EMMA

THE QUESTION HUNG in the air like a cloud that blotted out the sun.

"Emma, are you there?" my best friend Jessie asked, breaking the silence that had fallen upon our conversation. However, that wasn't the question that hijacked my thoughts.

Breaking from that trance, I said, "Yes, I'm here."

"Did you hear me?"

Had I?

"I don't think anyone knows Aiden is coming back," she added.

And there it was. Aiden. I thought he was gone for good. Now he was coming back. I wasn't sure how to feel. My relationship with him was simple yet complicated. He was what some people might call 'the one that had gotten away'. Then again, it wasn't like we'd ever dated. He was three years older than me, and by the time I made it to high school, he was with Darcy. Beautiful, everyone thought she was stunning, Darcy, and I hated her. Mostly because she had Aiden and I didn't.

They weren't always together. The times they broke up, I had a boyfriend. And that's how it went.

"I heard the sheriff talking to Stanley who is retiring, and Aiden is apparently interested in his position as the chief deputy sheriff. Though I think Wyatt is too."

Wyatt was one of the deputies in town who had recently gotten married to a friend, Sadie. She'd recently come back from LA too. Though from what she'd said, she and Aiden hadn't crossed paths there. While Wyatt had spent his entire police career in town, Aiden had left, gone to college, and ended up in the LAPD. Was he really coming back? I was engaged. It shouldn't matter to me, but it did.

"Emma," she said.

My mind had drifted again. "I'm here."

"Are you really?"

"I am. Promise," I said.

"Okay. Why don't you tell me how it's going with Evan's visit?" she asked.

That was a good question. Here I was in town having brought my fiancé to meet my dad in person and I wasn't sure how I felt, especially after how horrible dinner had gone.

"I don't know," I mumbled.

"Okay," she said, slowly as if every syllable was its own word.

I sighed before finally admitting what I'd been thinking about all evening. "It was supposed to be a perfect night, but it was a disaster." That was an understatement.

"Oh crap. What happened?"

"What didn't?" The incident had left a bitter taste in my mouth. "I'm pretty sure they hate each other."

"The two most important men in your life?" she asked.

One important man, I was beginning to realize. My dad would always be the man in my life. My fiancé, I wasn't so sure about. How much did I really know about him after all the things he'd said tonight? "I'm not so sure anymore."

"About what... or who?"

There was a knock on my bedroom door, and I glanced up. Evan peered in. "Can I come in?"

I nodded and said, "I have to call you back."

"Use your inner superwoman," she said, reminding me what I'd told her when she'd begun dating Miles, the hot new doctor in town.

"Wait..." I heard her say a second too late as I hit the end button. Evan slipped into my room with the widest grin on his face. Something that had once sent tingles down my spine, tonight, sent a shiver through me, and not a good one.

Schooling my features, I managed a mild smile. "You know you aren't supposed to be in here."

He slid in next to me, forcing me to move to the center of the bed to accommodate him. "It's been a week and I don't think I can keep my hands off of you any longer."

Hands that had brought me pleasure now made me cringe as he brushed them over my skin. I found myself worming away and forcing a giggle to cover my unease.

"We can't," I insisted.

"Why not? The old man is downstairs."

The frost that covered my features was instant. "That old man is my dad, and you owe him respect."

"Respect?" he spat. "His views are archaic. He can't possible believe I'm not tapping that."

His gaze landed at the juncture between my legs before winking at me. I rolled until I was on my feet creating more distance between us.

"That may or may not be true, but Dad ask us to respect

his rule of law in his house. And if you can't respect that, you should leave now."

I caught his flash of anger before it was gone. Just as quickly, he softened his features and got to his feet as well. "I'm sorry, Emma. It's just that I love you so damn much," he pleaded. "It's hard to keep my hands off you."

If his name were Pinocchio, his nose would have grown at least a foot in length. As he'd spoken, he'd inched his way in front of me. By then, his expression resembled the man I'd fallen in love with.

"Emma, it's me." He leaned in and pressed a gentle kiss to my lips before stepping back. "I promise, I will follow the rules." His hands were in front of him and in that moment, he looked cute and sweet all wrapped in one. He licked his lips. "Dare I ask, you leave with me tonight. We go back to my apartment in the city."

Seeing him like this, I was tempted, but I shook my head. "I need to talk to Dad."

Evan's lease in Billings was ending soon. He was moving back to Chicago after graduation. I was supposed to go with him. It was another reason he came to meet my dad.

"Tonight?" he asked.

"No. I'll talk to him tomorrow. It's important to me that you two get along. He's the only family I have."

He nodded. "I'll talk to him too and apologize."

I bit my lip to stop my grin. "Thank you."

He smiled back before leaving my room. I sat on my bed and looked around my childhood room. The one I hadn't left after graduating high school and had only redecorated to make it more adult. It would always be my home. I hadn't gone off to college but stayed in town and worked my way through community college. I'd met Evan at a coffee shop between our respective schools and fallen in love, or so I thought. I'd told my dad after the wedding, I was moving to Chicago, Evan's home. I'd been so sure. Now I wasn't

Maybe it was fear that was making me doubt my decision. Maybe it was hearing Aiden's name that had rattled me. Would Aiden move back to town with a wife? Though I hadn't heard he'd gotten married. Then again, his parents didn't come to town often. I'd kept my questions to Alana, his sister, to a minimum. She rarely talked about him.

But just because I'd loved Aiden from afar all these years didn't mean he would ever live up to the fantasy in my head. So why did it matter? I was in love with Evan, wasn't I? I would be married to him soon and whatever fantasy I'd have of being with Aiden would end for good.

I closed my eyes to vanquish thoughts of Aiden from my mind. Everything would change when I opened my eyes the next day.

TWO
AIDEN

MASON CREEK. There was nothing like the hills and valleys of Montana. Even the air was different here. A freshly fertilized field on a hot summer day smelled better than any day on the streets of a big city.

When I left for college, I never thought I'd be back, not to live anyway. But the saying that the grass isn't always greener on the other side couldn't be truer. All my life I wanted to leave and see the world. After college, it had only taken me a few years to realize how foolhardy that choice had been.

A couple of years on the fast track to become a LAPD detective wasn't enough to keep me there. I'd seen too much that had me turning in my resignation even before I'd gotten the job with the Mason Creek's Sheriff's department.

It was much more than that. Not that I was sentimental, but Mason Creek was home. I hadn't come back to work on my father's farm. I had been hired as the new chief deputy sheriff, the highest-ranking appointed position under the sheriff. I'd heard Wyatt, my friend from school, who due to a football injury had remained in town and become a deputy, had been interested in the position. I hoped there wouldn't be bad blood. We'd have to have a beer and chat about it.

There were a couple of things we could talk about. I'd heard he was married with a kid on the way. So much had changed since I'd left.

There was another reason for coming home or rather one person I was looking forward to seeing. Emma Hawkins. Though, according to my sister, Alana, she was engaged. That should have me looking the other way. Truth was, because of that this could be my last chance with the one that had gotten away. Wasn't she just that?

Alana thought Emma's fiancé was a creep. It was just another reason I wouldn't pull punches when I let her know I was interested in pursuing something with her.

What I hadn't expected when I parked on Tucker Lane, close to the town square, was for the streets to be so quiet. It was as if everyone was at a council meeting or had disappeared.

As I got out of my car, the doors to the church audibly opened behind me. I turned to see people spilling out wearing dark clothing.

Had that been why my mother had called a week ago? I hadn't called her back because I had an investigation to wrap up and an apartment to pack, then I forgot about her call.

I watched six men carry out a coffin on their shoulders. Behind them was Emma with someone at her side.

There was only one person's funeral Emma would be at the center of. Her father's.

Everyone headed to the right side of the church away from me toward the cemetery, except for one person. Alana saw me and veered in my direction.

"A little late," she said when she reached me.

"Nice shoes," I teased. This was one occasion she hadn't worn converse.

She rolled her eyes. "I'm at a funeral, and as much as I like those sneakers, I wouldn't wear them to a funeral. Now, why are you wearing that?" She gestured.

My button-down was flannel and not black. Neither were my jeans. "I didn't know."

She gaped at me. "How could you not? Mom said she was going to tell you."

"I missed her call and forgot to call her back."

She hustled me around the corner out of sight. "I suggest you leave before everyone gets to talking about you not going to the funeral." If I thought she was done, I was wrong. "By the way, just because you're here now, doesn't mean you start hovering and acting all big brother-like. I'm not twelve anymore. Mom and Dad accepted that and so should you."

I smiled and feigned ignorance. "What? I should pretend I don't have a sister?"

"Pretty much. Stay out of my business and I'll stay out of yours."

"Sunday dinners with Mom and Dad?"

"Not a guarantee. I have a job and college. I can't spend all my free time with family."

I arched a brow.

"You know what I mean. I'm busy, adulting. Now get out of here."

To her dismay, I had to follow her back towards the church because that's where my car was parked. I got in and from Tucker Lane drove down Harbor Street, turning on Mason Creek road out to the house I purchased from Stanley, the former chief deputy sheriff. It was a corner lot on

9

the edge of town with unobstructed views of the mountains. The land on the other side of the street would never be developed as it belonged to my family. I was close to the farm but far enough away; it would take a short drive or a long walk to reach their house.

What I didn't expect to find was Darcy, my ex-girlfriend from high school, sitting on my porch.

I took off my Stetson hat and ran a hand through my hair when I reached her.

"To what do I owe the pleasure?" I asked her.

She stood, sweeping her dark hair to one side with her hand without once taking her even darker eyes off me. The black dress she wore fit her just right. Buttons ran down the center on purpose knowing her. My guess was so she could leave enough open at the top and bottom to get a guy to glance her way. Especially when everything was belted at the waist to show just how tiny it was. She still looked good. Too bad for her, it didn't change a thing between us.

"You still look good, cowboy. I see city life didn't change you." Her eyes offered more than a hello and I just couldn't go there.

"You aren't at the funeral?" I asked.

"Emma might have died if I showed up considering her dad had eyes for me."

Darcy liked to flirt, and what guy wouldn't appreciate her attention? "Who in this town didn't?" I asked.

"Apparently, you. You left me for college and that was it."

Darcy had been my first long-term girlfriend, and we'd shared a lot of other firsts. But she wanted a commitment I couldn't give when I left for college. As much as I cared for her, I hadn't loved her like a man should love a future wife. It wasn't because she was wild and carefree. That was what had made our relationship fun. The problem was there had always been someone else I saw as my future wife, and I didn't think it was fair for Darcy to live in her shadow.

"We both know neither of us would have stuck to a long-distance relationship," I said.

She didn't argue. "Now you're back," she said, sliding her palms up my chest to my shoulders.

I caught her wrist and pulled her hands away. "Let's not start."

"Why not? Emma's engaged to be married. You can give up that puppy crush you have on her."

I'd never lied to Darcy, ever. "She's not married yet."

She rolled her eyes like I was foolish in my thinking. "He's rich and giving her everything a small-town cop can't."

I arched a brow. "Jealous?"

"Why would I be jealous of her? I've had the one thing she hasn't."

I took the bait and asked, "What's that?"

"You."

"Darcy," I warned. "It's never going to happen."

"Why? Because I was hurt when you left and did things I thought would hurt you?"

Word had come to me while I was in college about her antics. It hadn't bothered me in the way she'd hoped, letting me know I'd made the right decision. "You only hurt yourself."

She looked away and waved a hand. "No matter. I'll be announcing my engagement to the mayor by the end of the year."

"You're involved with Malcolm Wright?" He was older than me by several years, so I didn't know him very well. He had a reputation that rivaled Darcy's.

"Of a sort. He'll come to the right conclusion. We are of the same mind. Who better to marry than someone who will overlook his eventual indiscretions?"

I didn't think Malcolm was looking to settle down. So I took her comments to be fanciful thoughts or a way to make me jealous. Still, I cared about her. If true, I didn't want to see her hurt. "And you'd be okay with that?" She acted tough, but I knew her better than she thought. She deserved love better than Malcolm or I could give her.

"Of course, as I would have my own indiscretions."

It sounded like a world of trouble in my opinion, but it wasn't my business. Yet, I said, "There's a guy out there that will put you on a pedestal if you'd just slow down and see him."

"For you, I'd be downright virginal."

I chuckled. "Not me, Darcy. Someone else will adore you in ways I can't." She frowned and I blew out a breath. "I don't want to hurt you."

She stepped back and waved me off. "I was only teasing. Anyway, I came here to offer you my services."

I gave her a weary look.

"Ah, not that." Her eyes swept up and down. "Although I admit, you were a natural in bed." Her eyes lingered on my crotch. "How much skill or just damn luck to be blessed with a dick like yours, I might never know."

"Darcy."

"Oh, don't be such a prude. A girl can reminisce. Anyway, I heard you were buying this place and I know it needs work." She was in business mode, and I relaxed.

"I'm aware."

"And we both know you may be good with your hands." Her eyes met mine knowingly. "But you don't have a lick that will stick when it comes to decorating."

12

After she said lick, she seductively touched her tongue to her top lip before moving on. Malcolm had met his match. If I were a weaker man, I would haul her up and into the house. But I wasn't a stupid man. If I gave in, the town would know by supper that I'd bedded her by her very own words. Then any chance I had with Emma would be out the door.

She was right about one thing; I didn't know how to decorate. "Okay. What's your proposal?"

I'd used much of my savings on the house. There was no way I was asking my father for a loan.

"I propose a lot of things."

"Darce," I warned again.

"Fine. I'm just starting up my business. You'd be my first official client. I could work evenings for beer and a meal."

Her eyes held mine. We both knew what the town would say if they found out she was coming around. What choice did I have? My budget was small. And this home could be the beginning of the future for me in a lot of ways.

"This is between us. Don't use me to make Malcolm jealous, otherwise, I'll just ask my mother."

She touched her finger to my lips. "Ye of little faith. I won't tell a soul if you won't."

We shook on it. "Tomorrow?"

"I still need to unpack and don't know how long I'll be."

"Friday, then. That will give you the week."

As much as I knew this was a very bad idea, I agreed. "Friday."

Darcy was long gone when I sat on my porch enjoying a beer at sunset when a car pulled up in front of the house. I knew the car and the woman who drove it.

She got out looking as pretty as a picture, leaving me

13

swallowing my tongue as she walked up to the porch. Now wasn't the time to tell her all the things I'd waited years to say when her eyes were shadowed after burying her father.

I had to wonder what she was doing here and not with her fiancé whom I'd spotted holding her hand as she left the church.

What could she possibly want from me?

THREE

EMMA

Damn the man for looking so good. Tall, dark, and handsome as cliché as that sounded described him to a tee.

"Aiden Faulkner," I said, stopping at the bottom of the steps that led up to the wide porch.

"Emma Hawkins." His voice held the kind of bass that led women to make all kinds of bad decisions. "I'm sorry to hear about your dad. If I'd known, I would have been there."

"I know."

"I respected him a lot."

"I know. Don't worry about it. It was hard enough for me to be there and have everyone apologizing when all I really want is him back." I hadn't meant to cry, but I choked on the last few words. I'd looked down so he wouldn't see my tears, but then he was there.

Wrapped in his arms, he spoke words I needed. "I'm sorry, darling, that I can't give you that."

"I know," I said for the thousandth time. "I miss him." His shirt would be stained from my tears, but he held on. "I have no one left."

"You have me."

There was sincerity there, something that had been missing from my fiancé. He'd said all the right things today, but I didn't feel it the way I did with Aiden.

When I was able to calm enough to speak again, I pulled out of his embrace because it was too easy to find comfort there. "I need your help," I admitted.

"Anything," he said.

"You don't know yet what I'm going to ask," I said on a chuckle.

"There's nothing you could ask me, I wouldn't do."

I searched his eyes for calculation and found none. "You might want to take that back after you hear what I have to say." I held my gaze on his earnest hazel eyes. "You look so grown up in that cowboy hat. When did you stop wearing baseball caps?" Somehow, I managed a small smile wanting to lighten the conversation before I dropped the bomb on him.

"You like me in baseball caps?" he teased.

I laughed a little more because his smile was infectious. "You just look more official in the Stetson. I heard you're taking over as Chief Deputy Sheriff and you bought this place."

"I did." There was a moment of silence. "I heard you're engaged."

My mouth hung open for a second. "I guess Alana told you."

"She wasn't the only one. You know how things work in small towns."

"True. I don't see your parents often in town."

"Yeah, they keep to themselves."

As the conversation dwindled, he didn't press me to tell him why I was there, and I appreciated it. "I guess I should tell you why I'm here."

"I'm happy just to enjoy your company."

My mind was muddled with everything going on, but I thought he might have just flirted with me. I pushed the ridiculous idea away. I'd crushed on Aiden half my life, but we never got closer than being friends.

"My dad," I began. "The sheriff, the doc, they believe he had a heart attack and died." I met his gaze squarely. "I don't think that's true."

I expected him to give me the *it's just grief talking* speech everyone else had. However, he surprised me.

"Why do you think that?"

Shocked, I said, "You believe me?" Though I hadn't actually given him any facts yet.

"I believe you wouldn't have slipped out of a house full of people to come ask me for my help for no reason."

I choked on a sob again. To have someone listen without judgment was such a relief. My friends listened, but I saw their doubt even in their solidarity with me.

He hugged me again and ushered me to the porch. "Do you want a beer?" he asked.

"Please."

The door squeaked when he opened it to slip inside. I took a seat under the covered porch and looked out at the snowcapped mountains in the distance wondering if there was a more beautiful place on Earth. He returned and handed me a beer, taking a seat next to me.

"Why'd you come back?' I asked.

"This," he said, raising his beer toward the view I'd been admiring. "Growing up, I couldn't wait to leave. Then I left. There is a lot to see and experience, but none of it was better than home."

"Even with the gossip?" I joked.

"Even the gossip. I can't speak for everywhere. But in

17

cities like LA, nobody cares about anyone else. Your car breaks down. No one stops and if they do, you have to worry they have some agenda that wouldn't be good for you. I tried to make a difference. No matter how many crimes I solved, how many criminals I put in jail, there was always another bad guy, another murder, rape, or theft to solve. I was losing my soul there."

"Not much happens around here. Won't you get bored?"

"Maybe. But at least I won't feel like I'm dying a little every day."

I thought about that. "I have no reason to stay. I stayed for Dad and now he's gone."

"What about the bar?"

I shrugged. "That was Dad's dream. His slice of Mason Creek. I'm thinking about selling it."

"Can I offer you some advice?"

"Everyone else has."

"Don't give it up yet. Let someone run it and give yourself time to figure things out. That's the nice thing about Montana. It's not the hustle and bustle of the big city. It's slow, steady, thoughtful."

He made some sense. "I have another reason to stay." I sighed. "I want to prove my father was murdered." Once again, I held my breath, afraid he'd let me down like everyone else.

"Walk me through it."

I was grateful for his absolute trust that I wasn't crazy. "Ever since Mom died, Dad would never leave the house without telling me."

When I was young, I'd been home from school, sick with a fever. I'd taken a nap and it's believed that Mom drove to the store to get a prescription for me. On the way,

18

her car was struck by an out-of-towner speeding through a red light. I woke, feverish, calling for her. I'd been so sick; I'd passed out while trying to get to the phone to call Mom or Dad. My father found me on the floor halfway to the phone after being notified about the accident. Her car had been engulfed by flames, and no one knew if I'd been in the car or not. I didn't have to share the details with Aiden. He would have heard. I got to the point.

"We had a fight that night. More like he and my fiancé did. I'd been so disgusted by the pair of them, I'd gone to my room. I thought about talking to Dad and smoothing things over, but I decided to wait until morning." Guilt turned on the water works while I retold the story. "Morning came but he was gone. I remember thinking 'was he that mad at me?' until the sheriff came and told me."

"Who found him?" he asked.

"His assistant manager at the bar, Jack. He went in early because a truck was coming with a delivery. He found Dad face up behind the bar. He was cold by then, and Jack called for help. The sheriff was the first to arrive at the scene right after Jack."

"Any signs of struggle? Broken bottles? Anything missing?"

"No. Doc said there were no visible wounds beside a goose egg on the back of his head. It was assumed he had a heart attack."

"Did you get an autopsy?"

"No. Sheriff said it wasn't necessary given there was nothing to suggest any crime was committed. So I would have to pay, and it was expensive. I'd been a mess trying to navigate everything else, and I didn't know what to do. I had so many things to worry about. The bar, putting a funeral together, I just..."

"It's okay. I'm not judging you, Emma. Just gathering facts."

Though I was afraid to hear the answer, I asked anyway. "Was I wrong?"

"There's no right or wrong answer here. You did what you thought was best given the circumstances. Besides, we can still do an autopsy if need be."

I stepped back in surprise. "Really. Even after—" I waved it away unable to complete my sentence.

"Even after," he said, kindly. "Can I ask, what the argument was about?"

"You don't think Evan had anything to do with it?"

He shook his head. "I don't think anything. Just gathering information to help me determine his state of mind."

I closed my eyes, hating that our last words weren't good ones.

"Emma, no matter what happened, your father knew you loved him."

I covered my mouth as I began to cry again. "I'm sorry. It's just—"

"Don't be." He pulled tissues from his pocket. "I meant to give you these when I came out."

Grateful, I took them and dabbed at my eyes. "I'll never get to take my words back."

"We all say dumb things at times. I'm certain he knew that."

"Evan was being a dick, but so was Dad. I was caught in the middle. I told them if they didn't stop, I would leave them both."

He laughed, surprising me. "Your dad was always protective of you."

My laugh was without humor. "He was. He scared every boy away."

"That's not true. He put the fear of God in them, so they didn't treat you badly."

In the mist of sorrow, I could hold onto that. "He did, and I loved him for it. But how did you know?"

"Maybe one day, I'll tell you." He grinned, then the smile was gone. "Is there any reason your father would have left without telling you?"

I'd thought about that a lot. "The only thing I could think of was that Evan was there. Maybe he assumed I wouldn't be alone, but that doesn't make sense. He'd made Evan sleep in the back room downstairs since we weren't married yet. He told him no daughter of his would be sleeping in sin. That was part of their dislike for each other. Evan thought Dad's rules were archaic. His word."

Aiden laughed again and it wasn't at me. "Evan isn't from around here, is he?"

"Chicago," I said and laughed because Dad hated city folk. Not that he wouldn't have given the same rules to any guy in town.

"He already had two strikes against him."

"Three actually. He's rich too."

Aiden chuckled and tipped his beer back. "Where was Evan that night?"

I blinked. "I thought you said you didn't think he did anything?"

"I said I was gathering the facts. It's important in any investigation to get even the smallest details and not assume anything."

"I don't know. He tried to sneak into my room, and I sent him away. Then, I fell asleep."

"I'm going to need the names of anyone who has keys to the bar."

"I can get you that."

21

He nodded. "You should probably get back home before they send out a search party. Lord knows the rumors around town if they found you here. I wouldn't want your fiancé to get the wrong idea."

I didn't know if it was appreciation for his help or believing in me that tempted me to give him a thank you kiss, but I stopped myself. My mood would have steered my kiss to his lips instead of his cheek.

FOUR

AIDEN

EMMA HAWKINS WAS GOING to be the death of me. She was still as gorgeous as the Montana sky. Evan, her fiancé, was a lucky son of gun. As much as I'd wanted to win her heart, she needed something different from me.

The next day, I took a chance and went to the police station. I wanted to see the report the sheriff filed on Emma's dad. I walked in and was greeted by Bess. I was surprised to see her as well.

"Morning, Aiden. I thought you start tomorrow."

"I do. Do you ever get a day off?" I joked.

"Hardly," she said with amusement.

"Is Sheriff Moon in?"

"He is."

Damn. That meant I wouldn't be able to see the file without him knowing. "Is he back in his office?"

"He is."

"I'll go check in on him," I said and headed back.

I knocked on the open door and he looked up. "Aiden. Didn't know you were coming in today."

"Didn't plan on it, but here I am."

"Used to the city life."

I nodded noncommittally.

"Since you're here, I can give you the run down and tour of the department."

Our first stop was just one door down on the other side. "Here's your office."

It was a small, cramped office with a desk and two chairs in front of it. There was a small bookcase behind what would be my chair. I glanced out the side window.

"Nice view of the building next door," I joked.

"Yeah. You'll get used to it," he said before moving on. "Bess is here most days. When she's not, county handles the 911 calls and will patch it into one of us, whoever is here on call that day. Bess will send you the schedule."

"Sounds good."

We walked around the tiny station. There was a small break room in back opposite where two cells were located. We ended back at his office.

"How's Wyatt with everything?"

"You'll have to talk to him. I don't think he's sour about you getting the position."

I leaned against the door. "I just heard about Emma's dad."

"I wondered why you weren't at the funeral. I'd keep that not knowing part to yourself."

"Why?" I asked, truly curious.

"Folks will wonder why you didn't hear from your sister or parents. They might wonder if you don't have a good relationship with them. And you'll end up in that gossip blog by Tate Michaels. I think it's called the MC Scoop. My wife reads it religiously."

Tate, Sadie's cousin, had a gossip column. *Great.* I inwardly grimaced. That was new. I quickly responded,

"Mom called, but I'd been busy with a case and forgot to call back."

"Another thing to keep quiet. A chief deputy who can't be bothered to talk to his mother won't be trusted. If anyone asks, tell them you were late."

"But I—" Lying just wasn't in my arsenal, especially on something like this.

"I saw you when everyone came out. You were technically late, weren't you?" he suggested.

Anyone who had eyes would have noticed I wasn't quite dressed for the occasion. "I guess."

"Then go with it. Last thing I need is for my eventual replacement to start the job with people questioning if you are right for it."

Gossip was the main pastime in Mason Creek. And it sounded like Tate was capitalizing on it. I still didn't think it was that bad. I maneuvered the conversation to what I'd come here for in the first place and pretended as if Emma hadn't spoken to me about it. "You were there when they found him, Mr. Hawkins," I said, speaking of Emma's father.

"Jack found him. I was first on the scene."

"Jack?" I asked.

"Jack Riddle, he's the manager of the bar."

"I thought Doug, Emma's dad ran the place himself."

"True enough. But if Doug wasn't around, Jack was in charge."

"What happened?" I asked. I wanted his unvarnished opinion, so I kept Emma's request for my help to myself.

"It appears he had a heart attack and when he fell over, he hit his head on the ground."

"No signs of struggle? Nothing taken?" I asked.

"No sign of struggle. Nothing of value was taken,

25

including a small amount of cash in the registers and the money in the office safe. But... Emma believes the security disk was missing."

"Believes?"

"Jack said Doug often changed them. It's possible he removed it and didn't put in another for whatever reason."

"If he did, wouldn't you find the disk in the office somewhere?"

"We found a set."

"And?" I prodded.

"And where are you going with this? The man had a heart attack. We buried him yesterday. Let sleeping dogs lie, Aiden."

"Okay," I agreed only because I didn't think he was going to give me much more. "Did you check the other disk?"

"We did."

"Was the day in question on one of them?"

"No. But who would want to harm Doug? We don't have murders here every day. Not even every week or month. We may see a manslaughter from a car accident every blue moon. There was just no reason for someone to kill him."

The sheriff had made up his mind and I wasn't going to change it. But a missing security disk was reason enough to call Emma's father's death suspicious. I would need to tread lightly. The sheriff was well liked. Most people in town would know me or my parents, but I hadn't been around for several years. They knew the kid version of me.

I tipped my hat. "I'll see you tomorrow then."

"Eight o'clock."

I couldn't remember the last time I started work at eight. "Sure." Bright and early was my routine when I joined the detective division, sometimes as late as seven, but usually a lot earlier unless we caught a late case.

After checking my watch, it was too early on a Sunday to do anything but go home. I wasn't ready for that. Soon, the town churchgoers would be heading for services. As for now, the streets were silent. I strolled around the town square and familiarized myself with the businesses. Some were old and some were new. There were a couple of places I could grab lunch or dinner outside of the diner.

I'd rounded the corner and had passed in front of Town Hall when in the distance a tiny figure emerged from the covered bridge. The bouncing blond ponytail gave me pause. I leaned on the stone foundation that flanked the stairs up to the only public offices in town and waited.

My instincts were good. It was Emma and she jogged up to me.

"Hey, stranger," I teased. "Didn't know you were a jogger."

"I'm not actually. I spend too much time in front of a computer and need to get outside from time to time. I would walk, but walking means talking. Someone will want to chat if they see me. When I jog, most people leave me alone."

"Oh, sorry. Get back to jogging."

She laughed. "No, it's fine. You don't bother me."

"Glad to hear it. Do you have a second?"

"Yeah, what's up? You look all official." She touched the brim of my cowboy hat.

I grinned, hating the idea of bringing up her father's passing. "I spoke to Sheriff Moon this morning." When her face registered alarm, I added, "I didn't tell him you asked for my help." Her relief was obvious as she sagged some. "It came up and there's one thing he told me that you didn't."

"What's that?" She looked weary.

27

"He said you thought the security disk from that day was missing."

"Oh, yeah. Dad was religious about changing them. I wanted him to change it to a cloud-based system, but he didn't want to spend the money." She stopped, and I hated the sadness that crept into her expression. "Anyway, he had seven. He didn't think he would need to keep more than a week's worth at any given time. The one labeled for that Sunday was missing."

"Okay. I'll probably come in to the bar sometime this week and see how much I can get out of Jack without him knowing what I'm up to." Without an official case, I couldn't interview Jack.

"Thanks again. I know this might put you in an awkward position."

"You don't have to thank me. It's my job."

"It's the sheriff's job too."

"It is. And I'd like to think he thought he was doing you a kindness and not being derelict in his duty. Anyway, I don't want to hold you up. Evan is probably waiting." I smiled, though I silently prayed she'd say they'd broken up.

"Yeah. He's likely up, wondering where I am. And whether you like it or not, I owe you dinner, probably multiple ones."

I tipped my head. "I'll hold you to it."

Then she was jogging off and I took a minute to appreciate the view before continuing my walk around the square. As I made my way back to the police station, I was almost certain I saw the mayor leaving the only apartment building in town near the covered bridge. My view was from a little too far to be sure if Darcy was telling the truth. But if that was him, it made sense.

FIVE

EMMA

FOR THE FIRST time in days, I felt relieved. Aiden had taken me seriously. It had been worth sneaking out of the gathering at my house after the funeral to see him. It had felt like I couldn't breathe with everyone around. Even Evan. When I'd returned, there had been the making of a search party ready to look for me. I told them I just needed air, and they accepted my excuse.

Of course, Jessie and Alana had warned people off. Evan, however, had been suspicious. We'd fought about it, and I'd shut the door to my room in his face. I'd left this morning before he was up. Was I avoiding him?

The old Victorian house my mother dreamed of owning and eventually did was quiet. Legend had it that the man who built the charming romantic bridge out in the woods had a hand in designing the home. My father bought it for a song, as no one had lived in it for years. Until he died, he'd been renovating for my mother long after her death, knowing what the house meant to her.

Could I really sell it? I asked myself as I jogged up the

stairs straight to the bathroom and removed my clothes before getting in the shower.

I'd done a good job at holding in my emotions while talking to Aiden, but it was still too fresh. How could my father be gone? Tears streamed down my face when the curtain was shoved aside. I shrieked before realizing it was Evan.

He had a smirk and was starting to disrobe.

"What are you doing?" I asked. My question came out sharper than I meant it to.

He frowned. "I wanted to spend a little alone time with my fiancée."

"I'm not in the mood for sex."

"Jesus, Emma. I've been here for over a week and you've barely let me touch you."

Warm water was wasted as I continued our standoff. "I don't know Evan. You came here to meet my father and I warned you about his rules. He dies and all you can think about is screwing me. I think you should go home."

"He's dead. Nothing can change that."

Rage heated my cheeks. "Now I'm not asking, I'm telling you to get the hell out of my house."

He snapped back, "Call me when you're ready to talk like an adult. I won't wait forever." He spun on his heels and slammed the bathroom door before stomping down the stairs.

I covered my face in my hands and cried as a mixture of sadness and anger engulfed me. This shouldn't be happening. I couldn't imagine getting married now. Who would walk me down the aisle? I stayed in the shower until the water went completely cold. Then I towel-dried my hair and wrapped a fluffy robe around myself. I padded down the stairs and checked the room Evan had been using. His things were gone and for the second time today, I felt relieved. I checked for his car, and it was gone too.

I grabbed my phone and dialed Jessie.

She picked up, sounding groggy.

"Did I wake you?" I asked.

"Yes, but it's fine. What's going on?"

"Did I wake the Doc too?" From what I knew, they were shacking up.

"No, he's already up. I smell coffee."

"Does the smell make you sick?" I asked, knowing she was pregnant.

"Not so far."

"What has you up so early?"

"I can't sleep these days. Though I might sleep better now that I kicked Evan out."

"You didn't," she said, sounding more awake.

"I don't know. The idea of having sex with him makes my skin crawl."

"He wants to bump uglies?"

"Exactly, and all I can think about is the last conversation I had with my father was because Evan didn't want to follow Dad's 'no sex in his house until we get married' rule. And I..." I stopped because my voice cracked, and I knew my friends were tired of hearing me cry.

"You know it's okay, right?"

"What's okay?"

"To be sad. No one expects you to be happy now, tomorrow, or months from now. You can cry on my shoulder whenever you need. I'll likely cry with you. My hormones are insane. Plus, I loved your dad. He was one of the good ones."

"He was."

"No one expects you to be okay. Do you want me to come over?"

"No. I'll be fine. I think I'm going to take a drive to Home Depot."

"Home Depot?" she asked.

"Yeah. Something to do, and I'm going to make some changes at the bar."

"Do you want me to go with you?"

"Nah. Stay with your handsome doctor. I'll be fine."

I'll be fine, I kept repeating it to myself, hoping to make it true. I'd lost one parent before. Shouldn't it be easier the second time around?

Drowning in misery wasn't my idea of fun. I had to fill those spaces with action to redirect my thoughts. I hunted through Home Depot, angry at Dad for saying no to all the changes I'd wanted to make at the bar. Then I was mad at myself for being angry with a man who couldn't defend himself.

"Miss." I blinked several times until the cashier came into view. "How do you want to pay?"

I handed him my credit card realizing I didn't know the state of my finances. I transferred dad's written accounting into bookkeeping software, but I didn't know everything. *For another day*, I told myself. I took my purchases to the car and got in. I hit a random playlist and drove to the bar instead of home.

On Sundays, the bar didn't open until three to keep the good church going folks happy. The place should have been empty but when I walked into my father's office, it was anything but that.

"Jack," I said.

He stopped counting the cash and looked as surprised as I felt to see him there. "Emma."

"What are you doing?" It might have sounded like a dumb question, but what I was really asking was why was he doing it?

"I just thought with your dad..."

"It's fine. I can do that. I did it for Dad every day."

He nodded and put the stack of bills down on the desk.

"If you wouldn't mind, I'd hoped to have some time alone."

"Yeah, sure." He got to his feet but didn't go. "I know now isn't the right time, but I thought you should know..."

"What?" I asked.

"Your father always said when he was ready to retire, he'd sell me the bar. I know you're not thinking about that right now, but when you do, I'm willing to buy it from you."

I folded my arms. "You're right. It isn't the right time for this. Now, if you'll excuse me."

He tipped his head and left the office. I waited to hear the back door close behind him before I blew out a breath and got busy with a power screwdriver after I put on Dad's favorite songs to play through the sound system. Hours later, I stood admiring my handiwork. To the ceiling, I said. "I couldn't have done this without you, Daddy."

He'd taught me to be independent and not need anyone for anything including changing a lock or a flat tire. But he was wrong. I did need someone. I needed him. "I miss you."

My next task was to go through the books with a fine-toothed comb while I waited for the staff to come in.

The bell was music to my ears. I checked my new app and prepared myself when I opened the door.

"My key doesn't work," Jack said.

33

I'd known he'd be the first one in. He was curious about what I'd been up to.

"Yeah. I've updated the security system. From now on, everyone will key in a code to enter through the back door. There are also electronic locks on the storeroom, break room, and Dad's office. Why don't you come in? Since Dad valued you as someone he could trust, I'll share with you the changes before my meeting tomorrow with the rest of the staff." By then the other new equipment I'd ordered online should have arrived, thanks to overnight shipping.

We sat at the bar and I explained that I'd added more cameras and that the security was now cloud based and didn't need a disk that had to be changed every day. As I spoke, I watched him. Something just felt off.

"Also, I'm going to push customers to not pay cash. We are going to have less cash in the registers. Then there is the new inventory software that will come with the new registers I've ordered. We will be able to monitor how much liquor we should have on hand including what's in open bottles. The system will know how much liquid each bottle contains and the size of our glassware. No more comped drinks without it being recorded. It will be easier to know when to reorder stock."

"Wow," he said and shook his head. "Little Emma."

"I'm not so little anymore. Time to move this bar into the twenty-first century." Until now, the only change Dad had agreed to while he was alive was my suggestion to get new bar stools.

"Your dad would be proud."

That was enough to choke me up again. "I hope so."

I spent the next hour setting up each employee's security code to open the doors. They would only get access to the doors they needed. Dad's office was only available to me.

The bar was starting to fill up when I went up front to let Jack know I was leaving for a few hours. Jack wasn't alone. He handed Aiden a beer, and Aiden's eyes locked on mine. Damn him for being so handsome; and he wasn't wearing a cowboy hat. There on his head was a baseball cap sporting the name of our high school across it.

Instantly, I was transported to that first time I saw him, and my teenage girl parts had gone all tingly.

I saddled over and said, "Hi, stranger."

SIX
AIDEN

THERE WEREN'T many places for people to congregate in town. I went to the bar, telling myself I wasn't going to see her. She wasn't around when I entered. Jack was there, whom I'd come to see. I took a seat on one of the bar stools. As much as I wanted a beer, I had my first Sunday dinner with my parents in years. Mom would smell any hint of alcohol on me like a bloodhound.

"Beer," Jack said, like it was a foregone conclusion.

"Not today. Coke? In a bottle?"

Small towns made for judgmental people. I couldn't have people's first view of me thinking I was a drunk.

"In luck, I have a few in the back from the last festival. We get them for the kids. They get a kick out of them."

I vaguely remembered the bar had a booth at the festival every year. When he disappeared into the back, a few people I'd known growing up came over and congratulated me for being named chief deputy sheriff. None of them had been good friends of mine, so the conversations were short.

"Here you go," Jack said, handing me the bottle after popping the cap off.

"Chief deputy sheriff, huh?"

"Yep."

"Things are changing."

"How so?" I asked and took a sip of my Coke.

"Doug's gone. Stanley left for Florida," he shook his head.

He'd given me an opening. "I heard you were the one to find Doug."

His head drifted side to side like he could picture it. "I'll never forget that day. I didn't see him at first. I came around the corner and he was just lying there. Not moving."

I had to tread lightly. "That must have been a shock."

"Yeah." He ran a hand over his head. "I went to help him, but he was cold. So cold."

A couple of people came through the door, and Jack shifted to get their orders. I didn't want to spook him. So I finished my Coke, ready to pay my tab and leave if he didn't bring up the topic again, when Emma came over.

She smiled and came over. "Hi, stranger."

"Hey, yourself. I didn't expect to see you here."

"Dad would want me to keep living. Anyway, I was just leaving."

"Me too. I'm heading over to my parents' for dinner."

"Sounds better than my plan. Peanut butter and jelly for me if I'm lucky."

I grinned. "Come with me," I offered.

"I couldn't."

"You can and you will if you don't want Mom to kill me. Once I tell her I saw you, the first thing she'll ask is if I offered for you to come over."

"Will Alana be there?"

I chuckled. "I've been warned to stay far away from her business. So that I don't know."

She laughed too. "I can see that. Especially when you kicked the ass of every boy who looked at her. She had a party when you left for college. Not a literal one."

"I know. No party could happen without our parents knowing. Now will you save my life tonight?" I winked, then I remember. "Oh, Evan is welcome too."

She blew out a breath. "He's gone."

"Oh. Is that good or bad?" One corner of my mouth tilted up.

"You've learned from your sister?"

"I plead the fifth," and pick up my Coke only to realize it was empty. "Please come. Otherwise, she'll send me over with a plate."

She waved her hand. "Oh, the plates."

"Don't you have a lot of them?"

"Exactly. So much food shoved at me, peanut butter and jelly sounds divine."

"Your loss," I said.

"Except for your mother's apple pie."

I smiled widely; I felt the corners of my eyes crinkle. "You have to have dinner first."

"You know what, yes. I'll go."

I took out my credit card from my wallet and she waved my hand away. "Your money's no good here."

"Sure it is. And don't say anything else. You know everyone in town. You can't comp them all."

"Fine." She plucked the credit card from my hand and keyed the register. Then she handed it back to me with a receipt. "Sign here, please."

I added a generous tip and handed it back. She grinned then spoke to Jack before ushering me to follow her.

We exited out the back side door. "I can drive you," I offered.

"You don't have to. Then you'll have to bring me all the way back."

"Emma, it's fine, really. Gives me something to do."

I opened the passenger door on my truck and helped her in. My parents lived on the outskirts of town, but it wasn't that long of a drive compared to LA where the same distance could take double or triple the time. I appreciated there being no traffic around here.

"How's the house coming?" Emma asked.

"Slow. I've only worked on it yesterday and today. It's going to take time."

She nodded.

"It's good though. It will keep me busy."

"You sound like my dad. He was updating the house right up to the last day."

I didn't want her sad. "Mom loves your house." I thought I'd said the right thing.

"So did mine."

I'd put my foot in my mouth and remained silent the rest of the drive. I pulled up at the front of the farmhouse I'd been raised in. It looked the same as it did the day I left.

Mom was on the porch as I got out. Emma opened the door before I could reach it. But I was there to help her out. Mom's arms opened wide and enveloped Emma in a bear hug.

"Oh, honey," she said, cupping Emma's cheeks. Then her eyes found mine. "There's my son. Two days in town and this is the first I see of him."

She stepped in my direction, and I scooped her up. "You know I love you." I kissed her cheek before setting her down.

"Come in," Mom said, waving us in.

Once inside, Emma said, "I hope it's okay to come over unannounced."

"Nonsense. You're family. Besides, I always cook enough for extra. I never know if Alana's coming or not. And this one did a good job of eating us out of house and home."

"Mom," I chided.

"Go tell your father it's time to eat. He's out in the barn."

I tipped my head. "Yes, ma'am." Emma looked okay, so I left out the door I'd come in.

Dad was in the barn tending to our horses. We had a couple mostly because Dad loved them.

"Aiden," he said with a wide smile when he looked up.

There was a time when I had to look up to my dad. Now I was his height. We embraced and he clapped me on the back.

"I'm glad you're home. I don't have to hear your mother complain about not hearing from you. Now I can drive over and kick your ass if you don't call or stop by."

I laughed. "I never meant not to call. Just things—"

"No need for apology. You had a life to live just like Alana. Only with her, there's always someone in town who can tell your mother they saw her and she's fine."

"I'm sure they'll do the same with me," I joked.

"Maybe. I'm hoping you do a better job of stopping by." He held up a hand. "Not every day or every week. But consistently."

"I can do that."

"Good." He padded my back. "Let's go eat."

"I brought Emma," I said as we walked back to the house.

His brow arched. "She's engaged."

41

"I know. She needed a friend even if she wouldn't say it."

He bobbed his head. "She's had it tough. Doug did his best after her mother died. Your mom did a fair amount of cooking for the pair over the years. I can tell you she secretly hoped the two of you would have ended up together."

That surprised me. "Really?"

"Come, son. We have eyes. So did the two of you... for each other."

I opened and closed my mouth a few times.

He winked. "Let's get inside."

The meal was reason itself to come back to Mason Creek. Mom was a master in the kitchen, and I hadn't had a home-cooked meal like hers in a while. The few women I'd dated long enough to enjoy a meal at their places didn't have Mom's touch.

"Thank you for a lovely meal, Mrs. Faulkner," Emma said.

She held up a finger. "It's not done yet. I hope you have room for pie."

Emma's eyes widened. "Apple?"

"Yes. This morning I had a powerful urge to make apple pie."

"I wanted peach cobbler, but she wouldn't hear of it," Dad said.

Mom came back with pie and homemade ice cream. "It shouldn't be possible for me to have room to eat anymore. But I can't say no," Emma said with grin.

Mom served me a generous piece. I couldn't imagine why my sister didn't come home more often.

Only one piece was left when we were done. Emma declined taking leftovers. We were in the middle of saying our goodbyes when Emma said to Mom, "Thank you."

"Don't thank me, honey. You're always welcome."

"I know. Thank you for not asking how I was doing." Her voice cracked. "Because I don't know how I'm doing."

Mom rested her hand on Emma's. "Some things don't need to be said. You just know. I want you to know, that we're here for you. We can never take the place of your parents. But we can still love you like you were ours. If you ever need anything, you just let us know."

It was barely whispered words, but Mom heard Emma thank her again. Then she was hugging Emma who sagged in her arms. I couldn't imagine the pain she was going through. Guilt would have killed me if either of my parents had passed on while I was in LA.

A lot of eyes were red rimmed when we finally headed out. I left Emma to her thoughts on the drive back as she stared off into the distance.

Once we turned on the road around the town square Emma said, "You can drop me off at the bar. My car is there, and I need to close the registers soon."

"Can't Jack do that?" I asked.

"I haven't decided yet. Until then, it will be me." I pulled into an almost empty lot and she faced me before getting out. "I feel guilty about eating at your parents."

"Don't. Mom loved having you."

"It's just I have a fridge full of funeral food. I know everyone meant well and I'm thankful they took the time. But the idea of eating it makes me sick."

"It makes it real," I offered.

"Yeah. It's not like I don't know he's gone. I don't want the reminder. Not yet."

"I can take you to a shelter for homeless kids you can give it to."

She perked up. "Really?"

43

"I think so. I can certainly find out."

"Thanks, Aiden."

"Anytime."

She leaned across the seat divide and planted a sweet kiss on my cheek. I had the urge to turn and kiss her like I'd wanted to for years. I didn't. I could never be that selfish. Not with her. Time would tell if there was ever that perfect moment for me to make that move. She hesitated and I couldn't read into that moment.

"Goodnight," I said.

"Goodnight," she replied and got out.

I watched as she keyed in a code and entered the side entrance of the building. I sat there a second longer after the door closed fighting the instinct to follow and ask what had been going through that pretty little head of hers.

Just as I was about to pull out, Jack stormed out the door. He paced back and forth before pulling out his phone, punching in numbers and putting it up to his ear.

What was he up to? I needed to have another talk with Jack.

SEVEN

EMMA

THE AIR WAS CRISP, and my lungs constricted on each inhale of the brisk air. I pushed and ran harder like my life depended on it. In reality, I was working through all I'd learned.

According to the books and bank statements, Dad was doing okay. Nothing that would ever make him rich, but he wasn't in dire straits either. He was getting by like most folks in town. There hadn't been an influx of cash like maybe he'd taken out a loan. There was nothing I could find that would make him a target of sinister means, but I couldn't shake the feeling he'd been murdered.

I would have stopped by Java Jitters to see Jessie, but Aiden called and was coming by to drive me to a homeless shelter several towns away that was willing to take the food. I'd already transferred the food into disposable containers so I could return the countless platters and dishes the good folks of Mason Creek had delivered their comfort food on.

As I circled the town square, I thought about all the times I'd wanted to leave Mason Creek. Now I found myself contemplating staying. That would be the end of my relationship with Evan because he wasn't a small-town guy. I wasn't sure I wanted him to stay even if he was.

I turned onto my street and spotted Aiden's truck at the front of my house. I checked my watch, and I wasn't late. I slowed as I got close. He'd gotten out and was leaning on the cab when I came to a stop.

"Hey stranger. Funny meeting you here in a place like this," I teased, glancing at my watch.

"I know I'm early. I brought you coffee." He held out a Java Jitter's cup. "Jessie says hi."

"Thanks." I took it. "I like your hat by the way." He'd worn another baseball cap. I didn't allow myself to hope he'd worn it for me. "I'm going to grab a quick shower. I wasn't expecting you so early."

"No problem."

I liked the idea of him being there. The house felt too big allowing loneliness to take hold. As we walked in, I asked, "Sheriff doesn't mind you being late?"

"I guess I'll find out. I let Bess know, but the sheriff wasn't in. Wyatt said he'd switch shifts with me. It will be fine."

"I don't want to get you into any trouble on your first day."

He tucked a stray hair behind my ear. "No trouble."

His touch shouldn't have sent butterflies into flight in my stomach, but it did. "I'll be a few minutes," I said and scrambled up the stairs, hoping he didn't see my reaction to him.

I showered in record time and spent a couple of minutes debating whether or not to bother with lipstick. In the end, I went without it. He'd seen me at my worst already. It would be too obvious to put it on now.

"I'm ready," I said when I was going down the stairs. He

was staring at pictures on the wall and turned to face me. I grabbed the bags of food, but he took them from my hand.

"Let's go."

After we got into the car and secured our seatbelts, he added, "Apparently, children's homes have a lot of regulations, but some of the adult ones don't. I found one that will take the food."

"Sounds good."

Aiden turned on the radio and music played softly in the background as we drove out of town through the covered bridge. So many thoughts swirled in my head. "Can I ask you a question?"

"Sure," he said.

I needed a man's opinion. "If you were my fiancé, how would you handle the death of my father?"

He didn't look at me and kept his eyes on the road. "I would give you whatever you needed," he said.

"Like what?"

He tapped his thumbs on the steering wheel. I wasn't even sure he knew he was doing it. "I'd hold you, dry your tears, and wish like hell I could take the pain away."

"That," I said, fighting the burn in the back of my eyes. I wouldn't cry.

"Why? Is Evan not there for you?"

"Oh, he wants to be there for me if it includes us being naked," I said, swallowing the bitter taste on my tongue.

"Everyone handles grief differently. Just tell him what you need."

"You're probably right, but shouldn't he just know?"

He glanced at me for a second and I was reminded how many times as a teenager I dreamed of Aiden driving me home from school.

"As much as I hate to say this, he's not from around

here. He doesn't know you or your dad like I do. His empathy for what's happened only comes from wanting you to be happy. And who knows if he's ever had tragedy in his life. He might have thought that was the best way to get close to you."

I stared out my window. "Maybe."

Then Aiden took my left hand and threaded his fingers through mine. He said nothing even when I looked up from where we were joined and caught him glancing my way. I scooted across the bench seat, never letting go and rested my head on his shoulder. He let go of my hand and wrapped his right arm around me, driving with his left.

Being in his arms felt like a little slice of heaven in the hell I was living. It was the peace I needed, and I just allowed myself to enjoy the feeling.

When we arrived, Aiden said, "I can take it in."

I shook my head. "I need to see it through."

He didn't argue with me on the merits, only nodded. The contrast between him and Evan was stark.

As I walked in, I got an up-close view of how lucky I had it in Mason Creek. Tables much like the ones in the school's cafeteria were filled with people who wore an expression of defeat. How could I possible feel like my world had ended when there was suffering like this so close to home.

Aiden talked to a woman as I tried not to stare at anyone but still see.

"Thanks for this," the woman said.

"I feel like I should do more," I admitted.

"We can put you to work," she said.

I met Aiden's eyes and he nodded. For the next hour, we worked the line, serving food to those less fortunate. Though I'd been given instruction as to portion size, I found myself being a little more generous with the offerings I'd brought. The breakfast casserole was gone before I knew it. As much as I would have stayed to help at lunch time, Aiden had work. We thanked the woman and left.

When he got behind the wheel, he held out his arm. I slid over and resumed my earlier position.

"You know what I just realized," I said.

"What's that?"

"I have absolutely no food in my refrigerator now."

He chuckled. "We'll stop at one of those big box stores on the way home."

"Thanks," I said. "If I go to the store at home everyone will know I didn't eat their food."

"It's not a problem. Alana will appreciate me not coming into the store either." She worked part time at the grocery store in town.

We did just that. Aiden made me laugh as we walked the aisles and he pointed out the scandalous selections that would never been found in our grocery store. "Organic," he teased. "Isn't everything organic?"

I giggled and it felt good.

On the ride back, I was once again tucked close to his side with my head on his shoulder. I closed my eyes, lulled into a dreamless sleep.

Somewhere between the spaces of unconsciousness, I swore I felt his lips brush my forehead.

"Emma. We're here."

Slowly, I opened my eyes. I didn't want it to end. His arm tightened around me as if he could read my thoughts. "I can stay if you need me too."

Oh, how I wished I could remain right there, just like that with him. "No," I said sitting up. "You have to go to

49

work. I'll be fine." The last bit was just lip service. If I said it enough, I'd believe it.

"You will be. It doesn't have to be today," he said.

There he was saying all the right things that Evan should have said. And I should want to kiss my fiancé with the same urgency I felt to kiss Aiden. I didn't. I had more respect for Aiden than to involve him in something so messy. I needed to decide my future before anything else. Evan had a right to know exactly where my heart stood.

I gave Aiden my best smile, which was half felt. The better half because of him. "Don't be a stranger," I said and got out of the car before I did anything reckless.

EIGHT

AIDEN

My shift technically didn't start yet, but I had nothing better to do. If I'd gone home, I would have gotten caught up in a project and might have been late. I stopped at The Sweet Spot and bought a variety of pastries and muffins.

I walked into the station and the sheriff looked up from where he stood next to Bess's desk.

"Aiden. I see you finally decided to come in."

"I switched shifts with Wyatt."

He angled his head toward his office. "Why don't you come on back?"

Bess's eyes got wide, and I knew I was about to get my ass handed to me. It would be worth it. Emma had needed me more. I left the pastries with Bess with a few muttered words about it being for everyone before following the sheriff to his office. He stood at the door until I was fully inside and then he shut it.

He folded his arms over his chest like my father used to do when I was about to get reprimanded. Heading that off at the pass, I said, "I called Bess and she said things were quiet. I covered things by getting Wyatt to switch with me." I was repeating myself, but it was worth it.

"I don't know how they do things in the city, but here I'm the sheriff. I know I've chosen you as my replacement, but that doesn't give you authority over me. I expect to know what's going on in my station."

"Sorry, sir. I didn't have your number."

He rattled it off. "Now you do. So tell me, what was so important that you couldn't be here on your first official day at eight a.m. like we discussed.

"I was helping out Emma."

"Emma Hawkins?" he asked.

I bobbed my head.

"Helping her with what?"

"Not my place to say, sir."

He sighed. "I'll give you a pass. Lord knows that girl has been through enough and with both of her parents gone, she needs all the help she can get. Do you know what she's going to do with the bar?"

That should have been a strange question, but I chucked it to small town gossip. "No. Why would I?"

He shrugged. "She called you for help. Isn't her fiancé in town?"

"Not my business."

"Fine. I just thought she might have told you. Jack's making claims Doug said he'd sell him the business."

That annoyed me. "Doug's gone. It's up to Emma what she wants to do with the bar."

The sheriff cleared his throat. "Anyway, we were set to have a meeting with the mayor this morning and you weren't here. I made an excuse and rescheduled it for later."

"Sorry about that."

"Yeah, well, since you're here let me pass this on to

you." He picked up some papers from his desk and handed me one. "This BOLO came in this morning." As I read it over, he explained. "Apparently there is a brothel on wheels. A van fitting that description is said to be going all over the state offering good times for cash."

"Is prostitution a problem around here?" I'd never heard about it when I'd been in school and that was something guys would talk about.

"Not really. What we've got is a few women who trade sexual favors in return for helping them out with their rent or groceries."

"Is that prostitution?"

"Not when she doesn't specifically ask for a certain amount of money and just phrases it like she needs a little help without being specific, or so I hear. Most guys head a few towns over to the Lap Bar for a titty show and who knows what else. But it ain't my town, ain't my problem."

"Names of the women who skate the line in town?"

He grinned. "I'll let you find that out. Trust me, single guys like you will find out. Besides, if I told you, they'd see it in your eyes. This way, if they aren't skating the line, you can arrest them."

Great. That wasn't my idea of a good first assignment.

"Is that all?" I asked.

"One more thing. Rumors are going around town you hit the bar last night."

It was my turn to sigh. "I had a Coke. I bought a bottle so it was clear what I was drinking."

"Some are saying Rum and Coke. In fact, at first when you weren't here, I thought you might be nursing a hangover."

I groaned. "It was just a Coke."

"Why not get it from Java Jitters?"

"For the same reason, someone spreading rumors. I plan on buying a lot of coffee there. Since I was in the mood for Coke, I didn't want anyone thinking I was making excuses to see Jessie."

"The same can be said about you ending up at the bar. Someone else said they saw Emma in your truck last night."

I didn't think I would get used to the busy body nature of our town. I gritted my teeth, hating I had to explain myself. "Emma needed a friend. I invited her for Sunday dinner, nothing more."

"People are going to talk. Be careful. Not a lot of single women in town. These boys around here get territorial. You should remember that."

I was too disgusted to say anything about that. "Anything else?"

He handed me the other paper in his hand. "We got two BOLOs this morning. This is the second one. A missing girl down in Billings."

"Do you think they are related?"

"Could be. The state boys just want us to keep our eyes open."

I nodded and left. I sat behind my desk and hoped Emma wouldn't get backlash for being seen with me while being engaged. My detective hat was fully engaged. I had to put Emma's father's investigation on hold. The sheriff was too shrewd. In fact, it was looking as if I might have to go around him to get answers to my questions. In the meantime, I searched the database to get more information about the BOLOs until it was time to see the mayor.

An hour later, we drove over to the town hall. We arrived at his office in time, but his admin kept us waiting another ten minutes before we were ushered inside. He was setting his phone down when we walked in. He stood.

"Aiden Faulkner. I never thought you'd be a cop. I thought you'd be playing in the MLB."

"I turned it down. It wasn't for me." I'd been drafted into the minors with a strong chance I'd end up in the pros.

"Really, I heard you didn't get into the pros."

"I didn't. But even if I had, I wouldn't have gone."

"Then, why enter yourself in the draft?"

"No regrets. I didn't want to look back and wonder. When I got there, I realized that wasn't what I wanted in life."

He laughed. "If I had your arm, I would have taken it and all the pussy it would have gotten me."

"That makes us different."

Malcolm narrowed his eyes and then straightened. "Why don't we get to the point. Though it's Sheriff Moon's choice on whom to hire and fire, I thought it important we understand each other. This isn't LA. Folks around here aren't all bad."

"I never thought so."

"Good."

The sheriff remained quiet. Different was the man I saw now and the one I'd looked up to when I was growing up. He'd been part of the reason I'd wanted to become a cop.

"The sheriff also tells me you've been spending time with Emma Hawkins. How is she?"

I gave the sheriff the side eye before plastering a brittle smile on my face. "Good as can be expected seeing as she buried her father only two days ago."

"True. Can you tell me what her intentions are with the bar?" Malcolm asked.

Why was everyone asking? Then again, small town. But something was niggling at me. I couldn't put my finger on it.

"Jack Riddle has a real interest in buying the place. It would be good if you convinced Emma to do the right thing," Malcolm said.

"Right thing?" I asked, unable to hide the bite of my words.

"You know she's engaged to the city guy. Last thing this town needs is his father's company gobbling up businesses in town. We like our way of life here. Folks don't want a Starbucks on every corner. Do you understand?"

I nodded because I did. I didn't want Mason Creek to become more like a big city either. That didn't stop this conversation from grading on my nerves. "If she asks for my advice, I'll give it," I said without specifying what that would be.

"Good. Now if you'll excuse me, I have another meeting."

As we left, a beautiful brunette I'd never seen before was out in the hall and went in after us.

"Who's that?" I asked the sheriff.

"Probably someone from the county."

He didn't explain further. Considering I hadn't liked the intrusiveness of their questions, I let it go.

For the next few days, I also stayed away from Emma. She hadn't called either. I had gotten the chance to talk to Wyatt about me taking the chief deputy sheriff position. It turned out he had a side job as a handyman that kept him busy. He was cool with me getting the job as he didn't want the added responsibility with everything he had going on.

When the doorbell rang Friday night, I went to the door thinking it might be Emma.

When I opened it, it was Darcy with a Sauce It Up pizza box. I didn't know my smile had disappeared until Darcy asked, "Expecting someone else?"

That was when I remembered telling Darcy she could come over Friday to help me redesign the house. "No, just you." Because I hadn't been expecting Emma. I'd just hoped it would have been her.

Darcy sashayed into the kitchen where she put the delicious-smelling pizza on the counter. I wondered if across town Emma was eating pizza with her fiancé. Had he come back to town? I could have asked Darcy because in the past she seemed to know all the gossip, but I decided not to.

I was pretty sure I'd given Emma enough hints about my feelings for her. It was up to her what she wanted to do.

NINE

EMMA

DAYS HAD PASSED and I heard nothing from Aiden. It wasn't like he owed me anything, but I'd gotten used to seeing him and I hadn't seen his face the last few days.

The bar was unusually quiet even for a Thursday. I let my waitresses go, leaving me to wait tables.

Sadie, Justine, Leni, Laken, and Anna all sat around one of our bigger tables. I walked over. "Hey ladies, what can I get for you?"

They all looked at each other before Leni piped up. "Something for us to celebrate."

I grinned because their excitement was palpable. "How about champagne?"

"I can't," Justine announced.

"Me either," Sadie said.

The rest of the girls waited for either of them to say more when it hit me. "You're pregnant." There were rumors but I never wanted to assume. Both women nodded. "I'm so happy for you."

Sadie and Wyatt had finally gotten together, something I saw coming. Justine was blissfully happy with Tucker. She was there every time he did a set on my stage. Boy, could he sing.

"It looks like everyone is finding their man," I said, feeling a little bad for myself. I wore a ring, but I wasn't happy like I expected.

"Not everyone," Leni said. "I've sworn off men." She looked at Sadie and Justine. "But I'm excited for you two."

Laken spoke up next, "The only guy I've ever wanted, I can't have."

I could have said something similar. Though Aiden was back, he'd only ever treated me like a friend.

"How about I get you a round of cocktails and virgin one's for you too?"

They all nodded, and I left them. Was it wrong to feel envious? I'd thought I had it all until I didn't. Still the encounter with the girls helped make my decision.

The next day after spending a long time cooking, I took matters into my own hands. I gave hours to the waitresses I'd sent home earlier yesterday, which left the bar covered with Jack there.

It was probably a bad idea to show up at Aiden's unannounced, especially when I could have called him any day this week to express my gratitude. I hadn't. I'd also been avoiding Evan's repeated calls and texts.

What had I done instead? I made a pot of chili and drove the long way to Aiden's hoping the nosy folks in town wouldn't know where I was headed.

I sat in my car for a second before I got out. I lugged the pot to the door. The closer I got, I heard giggles. Female laughter. I bypassed the door to take a quick peek inside. I didn't want to bother Aiden if he had company.

There, leaning against the counter was Aiden with his

arms folded. Darcy Williams had her hands braced on his chest as she moved in for the obvious kiss. I pulled back before they saw me. I only noticed then Darcy's car was parked a little way down. It wasn't in front of his house as if she didn't want people making the assumptions I was standing on the porch.

I backed away and left silently. I didn't want to be caught for reasons unknown. I had a fiancé. Aiden was single and free to do whatever he wanted with whomever he wanted.

Just because it felt like he was sending me signals, clearly my addled brain had read more into it than there really was. For the millionth time, I thought I might cry. I sucked it up and used anger to stop that foolishness.

If Aiden wanted to hook up with the former home-coming queen, his ex, that was totally up to him. Just because he didn't know what she'd been up to since he left town didn't make it my business to tell him.

I drove to Java Jitters hoping to convince Jessie to commiserate with me. Only Miles was there sitting at a booth likely waiting for her to finish her shift.

I waited in line.

"Is everything okay?" Jessie asked when I reached the counter.

"Yeah. Just need my coffee fix." I kept the rest to myself. If I'd told her, she would have come with me. But the good doc looked like he'd waited all day just to spend some time with her.

"To go?" she asked.

"Yes, please." *Coffee for one*, I thought miserably.

When I stepped to the side so the next person could place their order, I caught sight of Alana. I moved in her direction.

"Taking a break?" I asked. Like me, she was taking online classes.

"Yeah. I need the caffeine to keep my eyes open."

I gave her a conspiratorial smile. "How about some chili to go with it?"

"You made chili?"

"I did and I need someone to share it with."

"Sounds like heaven and I won't have to cook. I can't stay all night. I've got a paper due."

After we got our coffees, I asked, "Your place or mine?"

"A break means a change of scenery. Besides, you cooked."

"It's in the car. I'll explain."

I waited until we were back at my place before I did. I got the pot from the backseat where I'd placed it to give Alana room. She followed me into the house. "Sit here," I said, waving toward the sofa. I needed a change of scene too. I wasn't ready to eat at the table or the kitchen island like I'd done with Dad. I set the pot down and went to grab us bowls.

"So who's the unlucky person who didn't get your chili? Jessie?"

I walked back in with bowls, spoons, and a couple of beers. The coffee had been an excuse. "Not exactly. Don't get mad, but I made it for your brother."

Her eyebrows shot up. "Are you and Aiden a thing?"

"No. Just friends. He's helped me out with a few things. I went to give it to him as a thank you, but he wasn't alone."

Her brows rose even higher. "Damn, he works quick."

"I don't think he had to."

She laughed. "Darcy?"

"Exactly."

"Stupid boys. They're like dogs wanting to be leashed.

But something tells me there's more. Are you and Evan on the outs?"

Alana and I didn't talk every day. She didn't know the latest. "I sent him home. He was being an insensitive jerk. Jury is still out on if that's a character flaw or foolishness."

"A little bit of both, I gather. He's easy on the eye, but..."

"But what? You've never said a but before."

"It's your business. I don't know. There's just something not right about him. He's a little too cocky. A little too city slick for me."

"You like your men a little rough around the edges like Cory."

She let her head fall back. "Don't mention his name. For all his promises, he broke every single one of them."

"Does Aiden know?"

She shrugged. "Maybe some, not all or he would have kicked his ass. Last I heard, Cory still considers him a friend."

"Would you ever go back to Cory?"

"No. Do you still have a crush on my brother?"

Boy, she'd spun that table fast, leaving me a little dizzy. "If I did, that would give me my answer as to what to do about Evan." I glanced at the two-carat diamond ring on my finger.

"Not that I don't think it's gross that you like my brother, but Aiden couldn't put a ring like that on your finger."

"I wouldn't want him to. Hungry?"

She nodded and we dove in. Alana caught me up with rumors around town she'd heard. I filled in with the little I knew because that's what you did in Mason Creek. You speculated on other peoples' lives. There was nothing else to do. Then, I drove her back home.

This was one of those times I wished l lived in the city. There would be places I could go, like the mall or the movies. Instead, I went to the bar and hung out in Dad's office.

The door was closed and locked. Anyone wanting to see me had to knock.

I got up and was surprised to find Aiden behind the door.

"Don't be a stranger," he said with a wide grin. I couldn't give it back to him.

"Can I help you with anything?" I said, holding the door handle.

"I could use your help," he said, hesitantly. Easily picking up my no bullshit vibes.

I exhaled and opened the door a little wider, giving him space to come into the small room. Aiden was a big guy. Bigger than my dad who hadn't been small himself.

Though I had no right to be angry with him, the simple fact was I was. He'd also done me several kindnesses. I owed him more than one. "Sure, come in."

He shocked me with his request.

TEN

AIDEN

Darcy turned to face me with mischief in her eyes. She was one of those women who was well aware of her looks and knew how to use it to get a guy's attention.

I'd been with enough women to know what I wanted at this stage in my life, and I was prepared to wait as long as it took to get it. Giving into temptation wasn't an option. It would only give me regrets I couldn't take back.

"What's in that bag?" I asked.

Along with the pizza box, she'd brought one of those reusable looking shopping bag filled with stuff.

"Don't you want to eat first?" she asked.

"I'll eat and you explain," I said.

"*First* you have to come over here. I promise not to bite unless you want me to."

"Darce," I warned. I had a feeling she wasn't going to give up easily.

She rolled her eyes before digging in her bag. "Come see." Out came some blue tile, a white square shape of stone, and two wooden panels, one white and one blue.

"What's this?" I did have a clue as I stepped forward but wanted to hear her ideas.

"The kitchen is the heart of the home. I thought you could go with white shaker style upper cabinets." She pointed at the white panel. "For the island and even for the lowers, you could do blue." She tapped the other wooden panel. "If color scares you, you can just do a blue backsplash in this tile and white quartz countertop which are easier to maintain than granite."

Then she pointed out how she would rearrange the kitchen footprint. It actually sounded good, though I wasn't that fussy. I was confused about one thing.

"Why blue?" I asked her.

"Personally, I'd go with grey, but I figured you're doing this for Emma, and I hear her favorite color is blue." My eyes widened. "Don't look shocked. I'm not dumb. You sure as hell aren't renovating this house for me." She placed her hand above where my arms were folded and leaned in. "Just because you might end up with little miss goody goody, doesn't mean you can't have a little fun." She came closer. "I won't tell if you won't."

I caught her hand and moved my head before she could kiss me. "Why do you hate Emma so much?"

She eyed her hands where I'd captured them. I let them go. She stepped back. "Why do you think?" When I didn't answer fast enough, she continued, "I loved you, Aiden. I would have done anything for you. You had to know that. Yet, you left me, broken hearted."

I reached for her, hating that I'd hurt her. I did care about her. "Darcy, we've talked about this."

She held up her hands to stop me. "Just answer this. If you had stayed, would you have married me?"

I closed my eyes, trying to think of a way to say no

without making her feel as though she hadn't been worth it. "Darcy," I said again, feeling like it was the only safe thing to say while navigating the minefield she put in front of me.

"That's a no," she finished for me.

"It's not because of what you think. We talked a lot about leaving. If I stayed, then that meant I didn't want to leave and I thought you did."

"Yet, you left, and I stayed."

"Why?"

"Where does a girl like me go. I wasn't great in school. Then, I really didn't have ambitions outside of marrying you."

"Really?" I asked. "The girl I knew wanted to see the world and you should."

"Who would want me?"

"Oh Darce, any man would want you. Malcolm doesn't deserve you."

"How would you know?"

"I met him, or rather I met him as the mayor today. I hate to judge a man on one meeting, but he's quite arrogant."

"He's my last option. God knows there's no one else in this godforsaken town who deserves me."

"You have a gift. Your ideas for the kitchen far surpass anything I would have thought of on my own. I would have left the kitchen layout as is. You should go to school or get an interior designing job outside of Mason Creek and find a man who will make you believe in love."

"Maybe I need to get over you first." Before I could think of a response, she went for the pizza. "It's getting cold."

After Darcy left, I took the samples and headed to the bar. I hadn't consciously thought of redesigning a home for

Emma, but faced with the truth, I had to confront it. I didn't know if Darcy was right about Emma's favorite color. Though I'd avoided her this past week, Darcy had inadvertently given me a reason to see her now.

What I didn't understand was the frosty stare Emma gave me when she opened the bar's office door.

"Can I help you with anything?" She stood in the open crack not letting me in.

What rumors were circling now? I tested the waters. "I could use your help," I said.

Though she looked reluctant, she opened the door. "Sure, come in." But I could tell I wasn't exactly welcome.

She waved at the chair and I took a seat after her.

"So what can I help you with?"

I opened the bag Darcy had left me. "I wanted your opinion about color for my kitchen." I laid each item out one by one.

She barely gave them a cursory glance. "It's your kitchen."

"I know. I hoped to get some advice from a friend. I guess I was wrong." I stood and began to pick the tiles up to put back in the bag. This Emma wasn't the one I helped a few days ago. Maybe she'd changed more than I thought.

"Wait." She stood. "I might be biased. Blue is my favorite color. I assume you plan is to do white upper cabinets and these blue as lower cabinets."

"Or an island in blue and white lower cabinets."

She smiled then. "I like all blue lower cabinets. One day, you'll have kids with sticky fingers, and you won't have to follow them around with a sponge to clean every surface all the time."

"Kids?" I asked.

She finally looked at me and her grin cooled some. "I imagine you'll have kids soon enough."

"You will too. I'm sure Evan wants a big family."

Her gaze landed on her ring finger where one hell of an engagement rock sat. I'd noticed it before. Her change in behavior had me thinking about it more.

She didn't answer my question. "Is that all? I'm sure you have plenty of other things to do."

I couldn't leave it alone. "Have I done something wrong?"

"Wrong? No. You're just you." I didn't like the look on her face.

"And that's apparently a bad thing. I won't bother you."

I shoved the wood panels back into the bag. When I picked up the backsplash tile, she said, "One more thing. I think if you have lower blue cabinets, you'd be better off with a white or grey backsplash or not all blue. It might be too much." She grabbed the sample of the quartz for the countertop. "If you are using this, I'd say go with white, but if you don't want that much white, definitely a light color like grey."

"Thanks." I plucked the stone from her hand. "Sorry to bother you."

"Aiden," she said.

I smiled or as much as one as I could and left before she could say more. Time for plan B.

ELEVEN

EMMA

THE DOOR SHUT with a finality I hadn't expected. I dialed Jessie straight away.

"Hey girl," Jessie said.

"I did something really stupid," I admitted.

"Oh no, what'd you do?"

"I went over to Aiden's house uninvited to bring him chili I made."

"Un huh, sounds diabolical."

"This is serious," I complained.

"Okay, I'll be serious."

"He wasn't alone."

"Now you have my attention. Who was he with?"

"Take a guess," I said.

"Come on. I have no idea—Darcy."

"Exactly."

"She didn't waste time. But I thought she was messing around with the mayor."

"Trust me. If she is, she's messing around with Aiden too."

"Okay. Now hit me with what you did. Did you bang on the door?" she giggled.

"No. I left. Went to see you."

"Is that why you came by?"

"What? Can I not come to see you anymore now that you're shacked up with the doc?" I jokingly whined.

"You know what I mean."

"I know. I'm feeling pissy. Since doc hottie was there waiting for you, I ended up hanging out with Alana. She wasn't surprised Aiden was with Darcy either... Anyway, he just stopped by the bar, wanting my opinion on a color scheme for his kitchen and I was such as bitch to him. I don't even know why."

"You're half in love with him, that's why. Not that I can blame you. He's aged really well."

"I'm engaged."

"Are you really? I didn't know that. I must have been blinded by that rock on your finger," she teased.

"Come on, Jessie. I need some advice."

"Pick one. That's my advice."

"You've met them both."

"Evan was cool the few times we hung out. He could have been on his best behavior though."

"For all I know, Aiden's not into me or he's not available. We haven't really had that conversation."

"I doubt that man is a monk, let me tell you."

"Not helping," I said.

"I can't choose for you. We can talk this through to help you answer that for yourself."

"Okay, hit me."

"I would, but we are on the phone. Maybe a good slap might help," she joked.

I laughed which was what she was aiming for. "Give it to me."

"Here are some thinking points. With Evan you'll have a cushy life, but not here. Evan isn't a small town guy. You marry him. You say goodbye to Mason Creek forever."

"Forever?"

"Forever. He'll claim there's nothing here to hold you back."

"My dad," I said quietly.

"I'm not saying you won't visit because I'll kick your ass if you don't. But it won't be the same."

I hated to agree, but I could see where she was going with it.

She continued, "And assuming you and Aiden had a thing, you know you'll have a nice little life here. He's not leaving. The man already did that and came back. He's made his choice."

"And I wanted to leave," I said, like that was a fact and I wasn't so sure anymore.

"Exactly. You've talked a lot about leaving. That doesn't mean you have to leave with Evan. There are plenty of men in the world. However, you aren't leaving with Aiden. I hope that clears things up."

"It does actually. I think it's time for me to call Evan. I've dodged his calls long enough."

"Good luck," she offered.

I leaned back in Dad's chair, which let out squeaked. Then, I dialed Evan.

"Hey babe."

"Hi," I said.

"Is everything okay? Are you ready for me to pick you up?"

"Not exactly."

"What's the problem?" he asked, like there shouldn't be one.

"I have to stay, for now at least." I needed to grovel to Aiden. He was helping me, and I'd been a royal bitch to him because I'd been downright jealous.

"Stay? We're getting married," he demanded. I didn't like his tone.

"I think we have to put our plans on hold for now."

"For now? What do you think I'm going to wait forever?"

"No. I don't expect you to. Which is why I think we should cool things off for now."

"You keep saying for now. If you do this, we're done."

Did he think that was a threat? "If you're giving me an ultimatum then I'll live with it. We're done."

"Wait. Baby, I get you're sad about your dad."

"Sad," I sneered. "I'm devastated. You have both of your parents. I have neither."

"I know. I know. That's why I want you with me so I can support you."

"I can't leave. There's so much I have to do. There's no one but me to make all these decisions I didn't expect to make. On top of running a business, I have to finish school."

"You don't have to. You're entitled to some time off."

"The semester is almost over. I can't quit now. Besides, Dad wouldn't want me to."

"Okay. What are we talking, a few more weeks? I can do that. I can come on the weekends," he pleaded, unlike moments before when he'd sounded like he hadn't cared.

"No. My head is a mess. I need time. I'll give you the ring back."

"Emma. Don't. Keep it. I love you, baby."

I wasn't going to say I loved him back. "I need a break, Evan. I don't know how long it will take."

"I'll give you a few weeks."

"Don't wait for me," I said and hung up before he tried to convince me otherwise.

It wasn't that I was choosing Aiden. From my discussion with Jessie, I decided to choose me. If that included Aiden down the line, I couldn't say I hated the idea.

On the other hand, even if my father hadn't died, I would have had the same conversation with Evan. I'd known for a while that I loved our adventures not the man. He'd taken me to all these new places I'd never seen. It was heaps of fun. But fun wasn't love.

I also couldn't sell Dad's bar. It was the last of him I had left. He'd loved the place. And for now, I needed it to help me with my grief. Being there, I felt closer to him.

My phone pinged several times and I ignored it. Evan gave up on calling and switched to texting. Was the fact that I had no desire to read his messages a sign? Then again, they say time makes the heart grow fonder. I didn't think so in my case. I finally realized I likely didn't love him enough to marry him.

I stared at the ring. I could take it off, but then everyone in town would get talking and some of them would demand answers from me. It was easier for now to leave it alone, so everyone would leave me alone as I tried to figure out what I wanted.

Still, I did need to make amends.

It was late, but not late enough. I walked to the front. "Jack, do you think you can close tonight?"

I had to trust someone, and my father trusted him. Unless I wanted to be shackled here every night, I needed help. For now, that was Jack. I prayed I wasn't making the worst mistake of my life.

"I need the code to the office."

"I know." I lifted on my toes and whispered in his ear. "It's Dad's birthday."

He nodded. "I've got your back, Emma. I hope you know that."

"Thanks."

There were camera's installed in the office now. I didn't have to completely trust him. And with the new electronic locks, I could change the passcode as I'd done right before I left the office. I didn't want to give him the code I'd come up with. Besides, he should know that number without having to write it down and someone else seeing.

The ride to Aiden's was shorter. I checked the road ahead and didn't see any cars. His was parked on the driveway. I got out and jogged up to the door, full of pent-up energy or maybe anxiety.

I briskly knocked on the door and Aiden opened it with a paint roller in one hand. He wasn't wearing a hat and he was also shirtless.

"Emma, I didn't expect you."

"No hat, cowboy?"

He ran his hand over his head. "I didn't think I was having company."

I rocked on my heels. "I know. I'm sorry." I peeled my eyes from the ground and met his. "I was a total bitch to you earlier and you didn't deserve it."

"You didn't have to come all the way over here to tell me that. You have a lot going on."

"I need to tell you to your face. You deserved that from me."

"Want to come in?"

"I don't want to bother you."

"No bother. Just painting." He stepped back and I went inside.

"I don't think I've ever been inside this place."

I looked around, wooden floors sagged in some spots and paint peeled from the walls in the living room. It showed its age, but there was a lot of character.

"Neither did I. I bought it sight unseen besides a few pictures sent to me."

"Really?"

"Yeah, Mom and Dad came by before I bought it. I trusted them to tell me if it was worth the price."

From the living room there was an opening to the kitchen where I'd seen him and Darcy. "From the little I see, it has good bones."

"Go ahead and look around. I've got to find a shirt. I didn't want to get paint on the one I was wearing."

"Don't get a shirt on my account," I teased. "You've filled out more from the boy down at the creek."

On really hot days, teens headed to a secluded spot where the creek filled up a little cove.

"You saw me there?" he asked.

"Who didn't? You didn't see me?"

"Oh, Emma. Who didn't see you?"

I slapped at his arm. "You acted like you hadn't."

He shrugged. "I wanted to hear what you noticed." He winked.

Not wanting to answer or leave, I asked, "Do you need a hand painting?"

"I'll take free labor where I can get it."

"Consider it a down payment on your sleuthing skills if you're still going to help me."

"Is that a question? You asked for my help. Besides," he

said, walking to the back. "Now that you're here, I'll pick your brain after I grab us both a shirt."

"Both?" I asked.

"That's too pretty to get paint on it."

"It's just a shirt," I said.

He held up a hand and left the room. When he came back in, he handed me a shirt. "Do me a favor and wear mine. Then I won't feel so bad when my brush accidentally slips, and you know." He lifted his shoulders and gave me a wide smile.

"Fine." I pulled off my shirt without a care in the world. The size of his eyes was the same size as the gaping hole of his slack jaw expression.

"Oh, come on. You saw me in my bra and panties before at the creek. You said. So what's the big deal?" I plucked the shirt from his hands and pulled it over my head.

"If you weren't engaged," he muttered.

"What was that?" I'd heard but I wanted him to say it again.

"Nothing."

"Mmm huh," I teased.

"Anyway, I learned a few things."

"What's that?"

"What do you know about the mayor?" he asked.

I dipped my roller in the paint and started not far from him. "That's an ominous question. Why do you ask?"

TWELVE
AIDEN

SEEING her in my shirt was a problem. Seeing her in my shirt and in my house was a recipe for disaster because she looked as though she belonged here with me.

"Aiden?"

I vanquished those thoughts. "Yeah. Sorry. The mayor."

"Yes, the mayor."

"I went to go see him with the sheriff and he was really interested in what your plans were for the bar."

She stopped. "Why?"

"Why, exactly. He claims not to want outsiders to get ownership of any of the local shops. I can see that. But he also brought up Jack as a potential buyer."

"What?" She shook her head. "I shouldn't be surprised. No one around here keeps their mouth shut about anything."

"I don't know much about Jack. What do you know?"

As she spoke, I ran the paint roller down the wall because I had a hard time looking at her without wanting to put my hands on her.

"Jack was Dad's right-hand guy, besides me. I know he relied on him when I was busy with school."

"Is he trustworthy?"

"I don't know now. Like I told you before, one of the first things he told me the day after Dad's funeral was how Dad was going to sell him the bar. I want to believe that maybe he's afraid I'll sell it without giving anyone a chance, but it did seem odd."

I agreed with her. "I hate to think anyone in this town is capable of murder."

"Me either, but something isn't right. I feel it deep in my bones."

"I won't give up. Though what I can do is limited. If I didn't work for the sheriff, I could act more like a PI. But because I do, legally, my hands are tied beyond asking a few questions. We need to get the sheriff to formally open an investigation."

"How do we do that?" she asked.

"I think at this point, we should consider an autopsy."

"You said they can do that."

"They can. The problem is it will cause quite the stir. Everyone will wonder. The sheriff will likely hate it. But it's your right."

She put her roller down. "How should we handle this?"

"As his living relative, you would have to request the autopsy. I can't as it isn't classified as a criminal investigation at this point. I'm not sure how long it would take, and it could be expensive like the sheriff suggested. But if the results show foul play, I'll be able to take more of an active role in looking for the killer."

"Okay. Fine. I'll do that. Whom should I call?" she asked.

"I'll find out and let you know."

She bent with her hand outstretched to grab the roller again but hesitated and stood again. "And if the results show no foul play—"

"Or inconclusive results," I added.

"That too. Then, what?"

"That will be up to you. I'll search until there are no viable leads. It would be great if you have a security system at your house that I don't know about to see what we could see."

She shook her head. "I would have looked at that myself."

"There are other businesses in town that might. That's something I'll look into. It would be easier to get that video with a search warrant. Time isn't on our side. I'll ask those that might have it as they might have caught your father's route to the bar or anyone else that might be seen going there. The bigger problem is the gossipers in town. The best way to get unbiased answers is if those I ask don't know why I'm asking. It would be best for me to get those answers before your father's body is exhumed."

"What can I do?"

"You can give me a list of business on the route you and your father take from home to the bar. A lot has changed since the last time I was here."

"I can do that," she said.

It was a struggle not to ask about her relationship and tell her she had other options, namely me. I dipped my roller in the paint when she said my name. When I turned to face her, I brought the roller brush around too fast and paint went flying. Splatter hit her face and hair.

"Oops," I said, but damn if she wasn't cute.

"Oops?" There was only a glimmer of retribution in her

expression before she flicked her brush my way. "Oops," she said a second time. This time a statement.

"So that's how it's going to be," I asked, sporting a smirk.

"Don't you dare," she warned.

"You have no idea what I'm going to do."

She didn't wait to find out. She ducked, putting her brush down and ran for the door.

I hadn't expected that, which left me a second or two behind.

Outside, she had her hands up. "You don't want to do this."

I waved the brush. "Don't I? You look good in paint."

"You'll have to catch me first," she said, taking off in the direction of my backyard.

I gave chase. Granted, she was quick, but my strides were longer.

Over her shoulder, she yelled, "That better be water-based paint."

"Wouldn't you like to know," I shouted, closing the distance.

She had no hope of winning and turned again, palms up. "Wait."

It was too late to stop my momentum. I took her down but managed to twist so she'd land on top of me instead of the other way around. The impact stole my breath, otherwise I would have laughed. In order to not crush her, the paint brush ended up in her hair.

"Sorry," I said.

She narrowed her eyes at me but hadn't otherwise moved. "No, you're not," she said with amusement. "Get this out of my hair."

I tried, but when she winced, I gave her the handle of the brush.

"Your plumbing better work," she declared.

"Depends on who reaches the working bathroom first."

Before I could roll her to her side and get to my feet, she rolled the brush over the left side of my face. "Oops," she said and leveraged herself off me. She was gone in an instant.

Now paint was in my hair too. "I'm going to get you," I called after her while laughing.

She was up the stairs, having guessed right where the likely working bathroom was. I reached the bathroom door just as she closed it in my face.

"My turn, first," she said. Her voice traveled through the wooden door.

"If you want to play it that way, you'll find there aren't any towels in there."

"Ugh," she cried, knowing I'd ultimately won. Yet, a second later, the water turned on. "I'll figure it out," was the last thing she said.

Now I was hard, painfully so as I heard clothes hitting the floor. Emma Hawkins was in my bathroom naked. Not wanting to feel like a teenager again, I walked to the hall closet where I stored towels. I got out two of the three sets I owned. I hadn't thought much about needing more for guests. It was a good thing I'd done laundry the other day.

I went into the bathroom attached to my bedroom and took in the paint job. I looked like an extra on Vikings ready for battle. I took a selfie to commemorate the moment. I'd probably delete it after I showed Emma.

I peeled off my clothes and turned on the water. I'd lied to her just a little. The tiny bathroom worked but the pressure was low. Pipes creaked as the water worked its way out of the faucet. I heard a scream and grinned. I wasn't sure because I hadn't tested, but now I knew that the plumbing was prioritized to the master first. I'd just stolen the hot water.

It took a while to get all the paint off with the water that seemed to trickle out of the pipes. I needed to call a plumber to get it fixed, but it wasn't a priority.

I was putting the towel around my waist when I stepped into my room. I wasn't alone. Emma stood there drying her hair with one of the sets of towels I'd left on my bed. She wore one of my LAPD T-shirts, which hit her just above the knee. The rest of her shapely legs were bare as were her feet.

She shrugged. "I improvised." She glanced down to where I was looking. "Thanks for the shirt. I assumed you wouldn't need this one."

I wasn't that guy who got hard when I saw any half-naked woman. If Darcy stood in my room dressed as Emma did now, my dick wouldn't stir in the slightest. Darcy was arguably a very attractive woman. Emma was different, and a towel wasn't going to hide my reaction.

"I uh—need to get dressed."

Emma's eyes widened. "Oh sorry." She bent and wiped away wet footprints before leaving the room. As she did, the damn shirt slid up her thigh giving me a flash view of the naked curve of her ass.

I groaned inwardly and sighed when she was gone. Only then did I realize she must have walked naked from the shower into my room.

It was late and I couldn't let Emma drive home. It was going to be a very long night.

THIRTEEN
EMMA

HOLY SMOKE SHOW. Aiden was a five-alarm fire which would explain why he was still dripping wet, or I'd have to call the fire department myself.

When Aiden came out of the bathroom with only a towel around his hips, I almost swallowed my tongue, literally. I covered the choking noises I made by acting like I was clearing my throat. He hadn't seemed to notice, thank goodness.

When I'd peeked my head out of the bathroom, I'd heard running water down the hall. He'd lied about only one working bathroom, but I wouldn't hold him to it as we'd been joking around.

I took my chance and ran to his room while he was in the shower to find something to dry myself with before he got out.

There on his bed I'd spotted a towel and snagged it. His shower seemed endless, so I'd taken it upon myself to rummage through his drawers for a shirt to borrow. I assumed he wouldn't mind given he was insistent I wear one of his shirts earlier.

After cleaning the floor, I pulled my jeans back on and tidied up the bathroom I'd used. That was where Aiden found me, bent over the lip of the tub scrubbing it with a sponge I found.

"You didn't have to do that."

I clutched my chest to catch my heart where it had nearly leaped out of my chest. I hadn't heard him coming. "It's okay."

I turned around and it was a damn shame he was dressed in a T-shirt and shorts. Evan had never looked this good.

"Have you eaten?" he asked.

Funny, I didn't know and had to think about it. "Actually no."

"I don't have much. I do have hot dogs and a pie my mom brought by."

My mouth began to water. "Apple?"

"Yeah. She dropped it by earlier on her way into town to take eggs and produce the grocery store bought from the farm and sold to the town."

"Hot dogs and pie, sounds like a winner to me."

I went downstairs after finishing and washing my hands. He was grabbing a bag of buns when I walked into the kitchen. I sat on a bar stool, resting my elbows on the table, and placing my chin in my hands.

"Do you cook?" I asked.

"Are you questioning my hot dog skills?"

"No. I'm just curious. I assume your mom did most of the cooking."

He handed me a plate with a hot dog and pointed at the fixings he'd left out. "I got a crash course when I moved out on my own. Buying takeout every day gets old."

"YouTube?" I asked, adding ketchup.

"Sometimes. More often, I'd just call Mom and she'd walk me through it."

"That's cool."

He looked at me then and I caught the pity. He remembered that I didn't have a mom anymore and hadn't had one for a long time. I waved him off. "It's fine." Though it wasn't. Losing Dad had also brought the hurt from Mom's passing back too. "Is that pie I smell?" I asked to change the subject.

Clearly, I hadn't known how hungry I was until I bit into the hot dog. It tasted like a slice of heaven. I moaned without realizing it.

"You were hungry," he said. I'd taken another bite and agreed silently to his amusement. "And yes, that is the pie. Mom thinks its sacrilegious to nuke it in the microwave. Thus it will be another ten minutes heating up."

That was fine by me. I gave him the thumbs up. By the time I finished one hot dog, he'd eaten two.

He checked his smart watch and I hope that wasn't a hint that I should leave because I wanted pie. "You should stay," he said.

I was stumped for a second. "Stay here?"

"It's late."

"It's Mason Creek not LA. I'll be fine getting home," I said. Though I'd broken up with Evan and no longer had an excuse not to find out what it was like to be with Aiden Faulkner. The boy I'd secretly loved half my life.

"I know. But it will make me feel better if you do. Otherwise, I'd have to drive behind you all the way home and who knows who would see me doing that and make assumptions."

He was right about that. "Or you could stay here, and I could call you when I arrived."

"I could do that, but you know I wouldn't."

I narrowed my eyes teasingly. "You wouldn't be black-mailing me, would you Aiden?"

"Who said anything about blackmail? Chivalry isn't dead, you know."

"Okay," I said, and angled my head just a little as I prepared my next question. "Where would I sleep because that sofa looks ancient?"

"You can take my bed. It's the only one in the house."

I grinned because I had a feeling where this was going. "And where would you sleep?"

"On the sofa." he said all innocent-like.

"Really?"

"Really."

"And if I said I could stay but we share the bed, what would you think I meant?"

"That we could be adults and share a bed to sleep in."

I bit my lip. "Do you have enough pillows to build a wall."

"In the middle?"

I nodded, while holding back a laugh.

"No, but I think I can keep my hands to myself."

"Do you? You couldn't keep the paint to yourself," I teased.

"That was an accident. You took it too far."

"I wasn't the one that tackled me." I laughed.

"You stopped and it was too late."

When our laughter subsided, his face got serious. He reached out and I swore my heart stopped for a second time that night. This time not from fear but anticipation.

His thumb wiped at the corner of my mouth. "You had something there."

My pulse raced and my face flushed. My entire body

felt like molten lava. I had to do something to stop all the physical reactions I had toward this man. "Pie?" I asked, breaking the moment.

He too had been in his head and I longed to know what he'd been thinking. "Oh yeah." He turned and got an oven mitt to bring out the warm apple pie.

Without me asking, he grabbed some vanilla ice cream from the freezer, and we ate in silence until he said, "Are you staying?" halfway finished with his plate.

It was a loaded question. "Yes. Though I think we need that moat."

That was my way of setting the rules. I wanted Aiden for sure. I didn't think it was the right time for us to act on our mutual physical attraction. We were friends and I didn't want to lose that with one night of stellar sex, if the rumors about his abilities were true.

"One bed and one moat coming up."

When the leftover pie was put away and the dishes done, I followed him up the stairs. With each step I wondered if this was what it would be like to cohabitate with the man.

With Evan I feared that we wouldn't last living together. We were so different that way. I had a feeling that it would be easy with Aiden. It felt easy now.

Without asking, he handed me a pair of boxers. I kicked off my jeans and didn't ask him to turn around. I didn't fear him. I trusted him. Besides, the LAPD shirt of his I wore was practically a dress, longer than some. I pulled up the boxers and had to roll them several times.

He just stood there.

"Don't be shy on my account. Sleep how you normally do. I don't want to ruin your routine."

What he said next threw a monkey wrench into that

plan. "I sleep naked."

If my inward self could come out, I would try to pry whatever hands were around my neck strangling me because naked, really. Naked.

"I'll just leave my boxers on," he said.

I didn't have words, I tell you, as I watched him pull his shirt over his head. Then he pulled off his shorts. He wore boxers underneath but not the kind he'd given me to wear that were more traditional. The ones he had on molded to his ass and his package. Holy moly he'd been given the lottery winner of DNA mix.

He pulled the sheets back and I forced myself to slip underneath. There wasn't a moat, but we laid there.

"Do you want the pillows?" he finally asked after a long moment of silence.

"I'm good," I said, not sure what to do next.

He did. His arm came out and he pulled me to him. It felt right to curl up to his side. I rested my head on his chest and listened to him breath. Eventually, I was lulled into sleep. When I woke, we were on our sides with my back to his chest. I lay there for a while listening to his soft breathing and wondered why I never felt this way with Evan, the only other man I'd shared a bed with in this way.

I eased away from him and onto my feet. I stretched my body needing my morning run. Though I could drive home and run. It seemed stupid.

So I put on my sneakers and left Aiden's house at a slow jog. It was different running here. The houses were widely spaced apart and there was nothing but the view of the mountains on the other side of the road. I found myself enjoying this better than running through town.

I nearly made it back when a car behind me slowed. A quick glance over my shoulder and I slowed too.

"Miss Hattie. Miss Hazel," I said when we all stopped, and Hazel had rolled the window down.

"Emma Hawkins, what are you doing way out here?" Hazel asked.

"Enjoying the view," I said, hoping they'd leave it at that.

Their blue and cherry red hair, respectively, shinned in the bright morning light.

"Did you know Aiden lives there?" Hattie asked.

They pointed to his house. I was grateful I hadn't parked my car right out front.

"Nice old house," I said, not committing to a firm answer.

They weren't buying it. "You know Aiden worked for the LAPD."

Crap. I was wearing his clothes. "Oh, this is my Love All People Dearly shirt. It's a PSA for kindness," I managed to say with a straight face.

"Lovely message. We have to go. We have a morning meeting at the church," Hazel said before driving off, but slowly.

I stopped at my car and pretended to stretch because I didn't have my keys. I waited until they rounded the corner before running into Aiden's house and grabbing my purse. I couldn't take the chance of them coming back to see my car still parked there.

Before I left, I had a moment of disappointment. I'd enjoyed my time with Aiden. Even if we were only friends, it had felt nice not to feel sad for a few hours.

I drove home in time to catch Miley who'd been at my door with a bouquet. She worked at Sadie's mom's flower shop, Blossom's Florist.

We met halfway up the walk. "These are for you." She

handed me an expensive vase with two dozen long stem roses. "They sure are something."

They were and could have only come from one person as I didn't think Aiden could have arranged flowers to be delivered so fast. He'd been sleeping when I'd left.

"Do I need to sign for them?"

Miley blinked. "Yeah, sorry. I was just thinking how nice it would be to get flowers like this."

"Not always I muttered."

As I scribbled my name on the paper she'd pulled out of a pocket while holding the ostentatious bouquet, she said, "Nice shirt."

I wanted to cry out because this would be news by the end of breakfast. "It's a PSA," I said. "It stands for Love All People Dutifully."

It was too late to take it back. I think I'd told the sisters dearly not dutifully.

I quickly traded her for the bundle and went to my door. I needed to get out of the shirt before my nosy next-door neighbor came out. But it was too late.

"Morning, Emma," Ms. Watson called from her porch. "Late night? I didn't see your car come home last night."

"Busy at the bar," I said and pushed through my front door.

I dumped the flowers on the island. Then I thought about damage control as I whipped Aiden's shirt off. I also had the other one he'd given me. I put both in the washer and went upstairs to grab my laundry. I would need to return this to him. However, going to his house wasn't an option. Not if I wanted rumors of us to die down.

The question was how to break the news to Aiden that I'd been spotted in his shirt, not once but three times, and it would likely be all over town by midday.

FOURTEEN
AIDEN

EMMA WASN'T in my bed when I awoke and maybe that was a good thing. As long as that engagement ring was on her finger, she was off limits. I'd given her enough hints. I spent the weekend at home avoiding town, painting, and planning the next task to tackle in my renovation.

Monday morning I got dressed in my uniform shirt and jeans. I put my shield on my belt clip and my hat on my head. Then, I thought of Emma. She preferred my baseball cap. I had to admit, as I gazed in the mirror, I looked more and more like my father when I wore the Stetson.

I left and stopped at Java Jitters for coffee.

There was a line, as it seemed everyone in town wanted coffee right now.

"Aiden," a redhead called out. She looked vaguely familiar when she faced me, holding a travel mug.

"Janet?" I guessed.

"Yes! You remember me."

"Volleyball team?"

She bobbed her head. "Yeah. It's great to see you back."

"Thanks."

I turned away, but she stepped into my line of sight. "Would you like to grab coffee sometime?" I looked around and we both laughed. "Right. We're getting coffee now. But you look like you're going to work. Maybe another time when you're not busy."

"Aiden." I glanced up to see Jessie waving me over to the counter.

"Excuse me. Looks like it's my turn." I tipped my hat to Janet and walked to the counter. "Jessie," I said.

"Hey Aiden. It looked like you needed saving." She had one of those I *know something you don't know* twinkles in her eyes.

"Ah, yeah. Thanks. Can I get some of your java? I think I've got the jitters."

She laughed. "Funny guy. Did your late night cause your jitters?" She bit back a grin.

Had Emma talked to her about last night? "You tell me."

She didn't. Instead, she asked, "Any special flavor in mind?"

"Coffee-flavored coffee is good," I said, with grin and a shrug.

She laughed. "House brand then. Size?"

"Big."

She shook her head. "You've got jokes this morning."

"I haven't had coffee yet," I said, deadpan.

Her giggle made me chuckle. "Black or with cream?"

"Black will work."

"Okay. I've got you." She winked and I stepped to the side. Janet was gone.

Or it least I thought she was. When I left the building, Janet was talking to someone outside and rushed over to talk to me.

"Aiden, I'm so sorry." I stopped and didn't mask my

confusion. "I didn't know you and Emma were a thing. I'm so embarrassed. Anyway, we can still have coffee of course. Emma could come too," she said in a rush. "I should go." She hooked a thumb over her shoulder. "It was nice seeing you again."

She left me standing there wondering what the heck had just happened. I would have called Emma right then, but I didn't want to do it on the sidewalk in the middle of town. I got in my truck and drove a few blocks over to the station.

"Morning, Aiden," Bess said.

"Morning Bess."

"Sheriff wants to see you," she said.

I nodded. My call to Emma would have to wait.

"Sheriff," I said when I walked in my boss's office.

He sat behind the desk wearing a constipated look. "Close the door."

I did as he asked and stood there more certain now what he was about to say.

"I got a call from my wife this morning. Can you guess what she wanted to talk to me about?"

Even though I could, I waited for him to tell me.

"My wife wanted to know if Emma's broken her engagement and was now seeing you. According to her, there is a story in MC Scoop about Hattie and Hazel seeing Emma jogging over the weekend near your house wearing an LAPD shirt. Emma claimed the shirt stood for Love All People something or other." I couldn't help but chuckle. She'd thought quickly on her feet. The laugh earned me a glare. "Am I really to believe that's a coincidence?"

I folded my arms over my chest. "With all due respect Sheriff, the answer has nothing to do with my job."

"We talked about this—" he began.

"We have, and my friendship with Emma isn't really anyone's business. I won't apologize for it or change it because some people in this town have nothing better to do than gossip."

"Emma is engaged. I might not like the guy, but she is engaged. I bet your parents wouldn't appreciate word that you're having an improper relationship to be talked about during Sunday church service."

"My parents trust I wouldn't do anything to embarrass them. I hope in time you'll trust me enough to give me that benefit of the doubt as well."

He sighed. "The other thing my wife called me about is a vacation. She seems to believe now that I have you here, I could take much needed time off."

"What about—" I was about to mention Stanley, the chief deputy sheriff who retired.

"He was a good cop, but not a good leader."

"But he was the chief deputy sheriff not just a deputy."

He shook his head. "Sometimes I wonder if you grew up here. Politics. He would have been Sheriff but even he knew his limitations. When the mayor approached me about running for Sheriff, he suggested that Stanley be promoted to chief deputy sheriff so he wouldn't run against me."

I was surprised he'd admitted that when he was so annoyed with me moments before.

"So I need to know if I can trust you to handle things if I take, let's say, a week off. The misses wants to go to her sister's cabin up on Lake McDonald for a little fishing and relaxing."

"Relaxing for her. Fishing for you?" I asked with an arch of my brow.

"Fishing is relaxing. Can I trust you?"

"You hired me."

He eyed me but I said nothing else. "Don't make me regret it. You can go."

I left and went to my office. My call to Emma went to voicemail. I didn't leave a message. After I checked the log of the previous night's events, I headed out.

My first stop was to Mason Creek Dental. I passed by Twisted Sister Ice Cream Shack on the way. Hattie and Hazel were there like I always remembered growing up. They waved and I waved back despite being annoyed they did what they always did; spread rumors faster than social media.

I took a left on Laurel Lane and parked at the dentist office. Tim was busy, so I spoke to the office manager to see if they had external security cameras. It was a long shot considering the type of business. But their location on High-land Place made a good vantage point to see anyone in town heading to the bar. I hadn't spotted any cameras as I walked in, but I asked anyway. They didn't. I lucked out that I wasn't asked any probing questions about why I was looking for cameras. So I left.

My next stop was to the jewelry store. When I entered, I recognized Ryder. He was a few years older than me.

"Ryder," I said in greeting.

"Aiden Faulkner. I didn't think you'd be back," he said, as we traded hand slaps.

"Any more than I expected to see you. I thought I would be talking to your parents."

"They retired."

I nodded. "I noticed you have external security."

"We do."

"You wouldn't happen to have access to footage going back over a week ago."

"We might. Why?"

Though I knew Ryder, my investigation was secret. But I didn't have to completely lie to him. "There is a county BOLO on a missing girl. I thought I would check footage to see if I spotted any unusual activity in town."

"Is it someone from town?"

I shook my head. "But a family is in desperate need of leads. I'm just checking around."

"Well, I'm sure I can get you a copy. Can I email it to you?"

"Sure." I pulled out my official card and handed it to him. "It was good to see you. We should grab a beer sometime."

"Yeah. I need it."

I left and didn't bother driving to my next stop. I crossed Highland Place to the bar and crossed Mueller Lane to the entrance of Bumps and Dents Body Shop. I didn't recognize the man in the lobby wearing coveralls. He was polishing something in his hand with an oily towel.

"Hey," I said, and startled him. He'd been deep in thought.

"Can I help you?" His eyes took in my uniform shirt. "Deputy." He had one of those distinctive voices you wouldn't forgot.

"Are you the owner?" Last I knew, Jessie's dad owned the place. However, I didn't want to insult the guy if he owned it now.

He shook his head. "That would be Henry Phillips."

"Is he around?"

"He should be in back. I'll get him."

"Thanks. I'm Aiden by the way." I held out a hand.

He held up his to show they were grimy with the work he'd been doing. "I'm Tucker."

"Oh, you sing at the pub?"

"I do," he said, nodding.

"My mom heard you at the festival and couldn't say enough good things."

"Tell her thanks."

"I will."

He ducked down a hall and shortly after Henry Phillips appeared.

"Aiden Faulkner," he said, with an outstretched hand. "I heard you were back in town."

"I am."

"What brings you by?"

"You have external surveillance cameras around your property, right?"

"We do."

"I'm hoping you might still have footage for the last week or so," I said.

"Actually, you are in luck. It's a cloud-based system, so it could go back further than that. Can I ask you what it's for?"

I gave him the same line I'd given Ryder. "It would be a help to her family if I could rule out that she'd been in the area."

"Her parents must be a wreck."

"No doubt they are. Any help you can offer would be great."

He promised to get me a link to the files if he couldn't email them. I thanked him and left.

I was walking out when Emma's dark blue MINI Cooper came around the corner. She slowed to a stop and rolled down her window.

"Hey stranger," she said.

It had turned into a running joke between us. "Yeah, do

I know you? Only a stranger would sneak out of your house in the morning without a goodbye."

"Sorry about that. I went for a run and ran into the ice cream and gossip sisters."

"I heard."

She sighed. "I'm sorry. If I had any clue I'd be seen, I wouldn't have gone out in your shirt."

"Don't worry about it." I didn't tell her about what the sheriff said because it was my problem not hers.

"I hope you haven't caught grief over it."

I laughed. "It worked in my favor when I ran into Janet." I paused. "You know Janet, right?"

"Redhead and single?"

"Yeah. She asked me out. Jessie saved me by the way. But on the way out, she apologized thinking that we were together."

Her brow shot up. "Did you correct her?"

"Didn't have a chance. She did all the talking, so I didn't have to turn her down."

Emma's grin was filled with amusement. "Why would you have turned her down? She's cute."

I eyed her for a second, managing not to show my disappointment that she'd asked me that. "No reason. Maybe I'm waiting. I'm a patient man. Mom always told me not to compromise, especially when it comes to someone I want to call wife."

Her jaw dropped.

I tapped the hood of her car. "Anyway. I need to get back to the station before the sheriff puts an APB out on me. You're here early."

"Yeah. I have a lot to do before we open."

"I'll let you go."

She didn't have to go far. She turned right into the pub's

parking lot which was directly across the street from where I stood. I crossed back over Highland Place where my department-issued SUV was parked.

Emma still had the ring on. Was I being a fool for hoping for something between us?

FIFTEEN
EMMA

No man should look that good, I thought as I turned into the bar's parking lot. Stupid me had suggested he date Janet. Had he scowled when I said it or was I imagining it?

I parked and sat there for a moment. Did I really think Aiden would stay single for long with all the thirsty, single women in town? The tall glass of water he was, wouldn't last long.

Finally, I let go of the steering wheel and went inside. I wanted to get the weekend's bookkeeping done before Jack arrived in case we needed to talk.

After using my new passcode to enter the building and once again to get into the office, I smiled to myself for all my handiwork. "Thanks, Dad," I said out loud. I could never be more grateful that he'd raised me to be independent and not depend on anyone when I didn't have to.

I'd finished up the weekend tally which all tied out to the cash deposit for the bank waiting in the safe. I was in the middle of reviewing the security footage when someone said, "I figured you'd be here early," scaring the mess out of me.

"Jack!" I flinched, putting my hand to my chest as if that could slow my raising heart. I glanced up to find him standing in the doorway. I hadn't heard the tinkling bells chimes from my motion detector app to alert me of movement outside the side door to the parking lot. I'd been so engrossed with what I was doing.

"We need to talk," he said. Not waiting for me to invite him in, he sat in the chair on the other side of the desk facing me. He hadn't closed the office door. No one else was at the bar but us.

"Yes. I do have time to talk. Thanks for asking," I said sardonically.

"Emma, I'm not your enemy unless I have to be."

I lifted an eyebrow. "Oh, thanks for that. It makes me feel all warm and fuzzy."

He clucked his tongue. "I love this bar as much as your father did. That's why he asked me to take it over from him when the time came."

"You act like I wasn't here longer than you. I spent my days after school in this very office doing homework after my mother died. I don't even think you were working here back then."

"Doing homework is a far cry from running the bar. You always had one foot in and one foot out. That's why your father ask me and not you to run the place after him." His resentment rolled off him like waves.

"You want things to go back to the way they were before?" I accused.

"Yes."

"You want to run things while I pop in and out like when Dad was around?"

"Yes."

"Or preferably you want me to sell you the place and walk away?"

"Yes." His sneer had grown with each response.

I clasped my hands and leaned on the desk in his direction. "I'm sorry to inform you, I haven't made a decision as to what I'm going to do."

He didn't back down and leaned toward me as if we needed to whisper so we wouldn't be overhead. "Have you even looked over his will?" When I blanched, he added, "Maybe you have and realized he made provisions for me to take over because he didn't want your arrogant punk ass boyfriend to get his hands on it."

Any smart alec remarks I could have made died in my throat. He got to his feet.

"I'm going to do inventory, Boss," he said the title like it tasted bad. "If you don't mind."

I shook my head. Before he left, he turned back, and I waited for the next barb to leave his sharp-edged tongue. "I may not like your fiancé," he snapped. "But your father would be disappointed over how you're carrying on with the new chief deputy sheriff while you're engaged."

Gaping didn't quite describe how I had to pick my jaw off the floor after he left. I thought too late to call out and tell him Aiden and I were just friends. The moment had passed, and the line between Jack and I was drawn.

However, what took my complete attention was the fact that I hadn't thought about Dad's will. I'd gotten through the funeral and requested Aiden's help investigating my father's death. However, it had never dawned on me that Dad might have left the bar to Jack to buy or to outright give it to him. I had made my intention of leaving Mason Creek for good one day clear to Dad. So, Jack could be right.

The will wasn't here in the office from what I could see.

Unless it had been, and Jack had gotten his hands on it. I would have to go home to check if it wasn't there before making any more assumptions.

I grabbed the deposit bag and my purse. I closed the office door and didn't bother to check in with Jack. He'd made it clear I didn't need to babysit him, and I hadn't found any reasons so far to dispute that.

I drove over to Brandford Bank to make the deposit. On the way inside, everyone I passed seemed to glance at me, then at the sheriff's station next door as if waiting to see if that was my destination. I groaned, remembering Aiden's jaw tightening when I told him about Hattie and Hazel seeing me in his shirt.

Had he been getting the same grief and scrutiny I had even though he hadn't admitted it? Likely, and I felt awful. Last thing he needed would be labeled as a fiancée stealer even though no one in town would be loyal to Evan. I sighed and entered the bank. I hoped I didn't get asked a dozen questions about my relationship status while I was there.

Lucky me, I was the only one inside. The teller was young, barely out of high school. Based on her face, I was sure I knew her parents though I didn't bring it up. She seemed more interested in getting me out so she could go back to whatever she was doing on her phone.

I might have stopped by to see Aiden to smooth things over. But distance was probably better for both of us. Me seeing him now would only add to the speculation surrounding us.

At home, I went straight to Dad's office downstairs, the room we'd converted into a bedroom for Evan's stay. It was still a bedroom. I hadn't done anything to the room since kicking him out. The sheets were still tangled. I left it. Dad had moved some boxes upstairs into the spare bedroom to make room for Evan's stuff while he was in town.

Everything was boxed up, and I didn't think he'd have his will there. I left that room and went into his bedroom. I stopped in the doorway. The room faintly smelled of him and my eyes misted. God, I missed him. I forced myself forward and opened his closet. His clothes hung there in anticipation of being worn. I'd have to decide what to do with them, but not now.

I crotched to find his home safe sitting on the floor. I didn't have to guess at the code. It was my mother's birthday. Though that was an easily hacked number, dad wouldn't change it.

Inside, his gun sat on top. I pulled it out and set it to the side with the barrel facing away from me. I'd been taught at a young age all about gun safety. Then, I pulled out four stacks of bills. Dad believed in being prepared. In the event we had to leave in a hurry because of weather or any other natural disaster, he'd want to have access to cash. Underneath was a letter with my name on it.

I rocked back as a wave of pain clenched my chest. With unsteady fingers I worked open the seal as tears poured from my eyes.

Emmabean, it began. I choked out a sob and had to close my eyes before I could read on.

If you are reading this, I guess I've passed on and I'm sorry for it. Because otherwise I would be telling you these words while on my death bed long in the future instead of you reading them.

First, I want to say how incredibly proud I am of you and the woman you've become. Yes, you are still finding your place in the world, but I have no doubt you're on the right path.

I hope you find happiness as I did with your mother even if it's with Evan. It's the greatest gift one can have next to the love of one's child.

He'd obviously written this recently, I thought. Why had he been thinking about death? Had something really been wrong with his health? I continued reading.

I know you want to leave Mason Creek. I can't blame you. When I was young, I wanted to leave too until I met your mother. Then, I didn't want to share her with the world. It was safer to keep her here.

I smiled a little.

I never stopped loving her and I'll never stop loving you in this life or the next. Don't tell the reverend I said that.

Then, I did laugh a little.

My Emma. Your life is your own. Though I leave every-thing to you, you choose to do what it is as you want. The house, the pub, everything. Those things are your Mom's and my dreams. They don't have to be yours. I'll leave that up to you. Whatever you decide, don't let things hold you back from being you. I trust and respect you.

If I haven't said it enough, I love you, always,
Dad

I curled in a ball on the floor and cried while clutching the letter. My heart once again broke into a million pieces.

When my tears dried, my first instinct was to call Aiden. I didn't want to acknowledge that. Instead, I picked myself up and went back down to the room below to purge my house of any evidence of Evan's presence. I started with the bed sheets. Before I started the laundry, Aiden's shirts sat neatly folded where I'd done laundry the other day. I'd caused Aiden too much embarrassment. I would need to figure out a way to return them to him without the entire town finding out.

SIXTEEN
AIDEN

For the last few days, I combed through hours of footage I'd gotten from the jewelry store and the auto shop because I couldn't enter a day or time to find the segment I wanted.

The jewelry store footage hadn't gone back far enough. Though I did watch for vehicles late at night for the BOLO for the missing girl. I found nothing.

I hit pay dirt with auto shop store footage. On the night of Doug's death, I spotted his car go into the lot at a little past midnight. Maybe twenty minutes later, another vehicle passed the bar, but it didn't turn into the lot. The car disappeared on Highland Place at a slow pace. I couldn't tell if it stopped and parked before it went out of range. I made a note of the license plate. A quick search led me to a car rental company.

Since Emma's father's death hadn't been ruled a homicide or suspicious death, I couldn't compel the rental company to give me the name of the person who rented that car.

I'd sent Emma the information she needed to set up a

private autopsy a few days ago. I'd gotten back a thank you and nothing else. I hadn't seen or heard from her since. I had to assume she was avoiding me. Since I hadn't called her, was I doing the same?

Sighing, I scrubbed a hand over my face. I was tired and considering what I would have for dinner when I got a call.

"Cory?" I asked.

"Hey man. Can you meet me at Sal's?"

It was the name of a bar a few towns over. I checked my watch. My shift was nearly over, and I needed to eat. I would finish looking at footage later. "Okay. I'll be there in thirty minutes."

The place was more than half empty when I walked in. I spotted Cory sitting alone at a four top. I took the seat across from him.

"You couldn't meet me in town?" I asked.

"Everyone hates me," he complained.

The everyone he talked about sided with my sister on how he'd treated her. "What's going on?" I asked, because he had to have a reason to want to talk to me.

"I heard you were back in town."

That couldn't be it, so I stayed silent knowing he'd end up telling me the real reason.

"I thought maybe you could put in a good word for me."

"With who?" I asked, raising a brow.

"Your sister for one. If she forgives me maybe I could come back without being chased out of town with pitchforks."

Of course, he was joking but it wasn't far from the truth. I shook my head. "Can't help you there. Alana doesn't want me in her business. Besides, if I talk to her, you'll have to confess everything you did. And we both know I'll have to kick your ass. It's better if I only hear rumors and not the truth."

Cory had been a decent guy with a lot of ambition. His foray into the rodeo had buckle bunnies chasing him. Hard on a man not to fall when you're out on the road for weeks. That didn't give him a pass for breaking my sister's heart. It did, however, give a reason.

"I still love her," he said, like that would create sway in his favor.

"Maybe you do, maybe you don't. But I'm not the one you need to convince."

His shoulders slumped. "Come on Aiden. You're my closet friend. Who else can I talk to?"

"A therapist," I joked.

He drank the rest of his beer and waved a hand to the waitress for another. She came over and gave me all her attention. "Hey sugar, what can I get you?"

She was cute, but she wasn't Emma. "A beer and a burger."

She nodded and would have walked away, but Cory said, "Another beer, please."

I don't know what he'd done to her, but she scowled before taking his empty bottle and leaving.

"Women," Cory said. "Speaking of, what's up with Emma Hawkins. I heard she's engaged."

"That's what they say."

He eyed me suspiciously. "They also say she was seen wearing your shirt early one morning."

Fire burned in my gut. "You shouldn't listen to rumors. Besides, where are you getting your information if you can't come to town?"

"My parents still talk to me," he said, defensively. I didn't think that was his source. "So, is it true?"

"We're friends."

"That's all?" he asked with a sly smile like he'd won the lottery of information. "Because Emma is hot. I would have tried to hook up with her before but she's friends with Alana. I think enough time has passed where I could date her friend, don't you think?"

What I thought in the saloon style pub was drawing my gun and shooting him between the eyes for suggesting such a thing. But it wasn't the eighteen hundreds, and that action would get me the death penalty in Montana.

"I think if you ever think about Emma that way again, I'll kill you."

He rocked back on his chair and pointed at me. "I knew it. You still have it bad for sweet Emma Hawkins. How does Darcy feel about that? She's a sweet piece of ass I haven't had the pleasure of tasting."

"Darcy doesn't need your kind of trouble."

He sat back up, front chair legs hitting the floor.

"Darcy needs someone who will settle down and take care of her. You, on the other hand, don't seem ready for that."

"Come on, Aiden. I'm just yanking your chain. You wouldn't tell me shit otherwise. I still want Alana," he said sheepishly. "I really fucked that up."

"You did."

My beer and burger arrived, and I let him tell me about life on the rodeo. As much as I believed he still cared about my sister, he wasn't right for her.

When I got home, I called her. "I know you want me to stay out of your life, but I just saw Cory." I told her about our conversation. The parts that had to do with her. She listened and didn't comment.

"Is that all?"

"Yes," I said.

"Thanks."

And that was it. I hadn't seen much of her since I'd been back in town. She was true to her word of doing her own thing and I had to let her.

Later that night, I couldn't sleep. I sat on my bed with my laptop reviewing the security footage frame by frame to see just where the rental car had gone when my phone rang.

"Emma," I said.

She sniffed. "They're doing it now. I thought I could be here by myself—"

"You don't have to. I'll be there."

I took off the shorts I'd been wearing, threw on some jeans, and grabbed my keys. I drove the long way avoiding a drive through town and pulled up behind Emma's MINI Cooper ten minutes later.

There in the dark, a backhoe worked to remove dirt. I hopped out of my truck and went to Emma's passenger side. I knocked. She turned and moonlight lit up her face. I took in her red-rimmed eyes before she unlocked the door.

It was almost comical how I had to fold myself to get into her car. I was tall and the car was low to the ground. Once in, it was semi-comfortable. Better than I thought. I reached out an arm and Emma leaned into me. I held her while she cried. This couldn't be easy. I didn't want to imagine the day I would have to say goodbye to either or both of my parents. She'd done it twice.

I stroked her hair and murmured things like 'I've got you' as her father's grave was unearthed.

"It's going to be some kind of awful tomorrow," she said in my chest. "I asked them to do it late or really early, but people are going to find out."

They were and there would be lots of questions. I was

happy the sheriff was away. Though he'd hear about it even on the lake. Someone would call and he would call me. I wasn't looking forward to it.

"Am I making a mistake?" she asked, on a hiccupping whimper.

"You want justice for your dad?"

She jerkily nodded without pulling away.

"Then you're doing the right thing."

"I hope so. This is costing me a fortune."

I was angry then. "If the sheriff would have done his job, it wouldn't have cost you a thing."

She pulled away. "What do you know?"

"Not much. But he should have investigated it. The missing security disk was enough to question the circumstances surrounding your father's death. Doing an autopsy then would have given answers that we might not get now."

"You haven't found anything else?"

Because we hadn't spoken, I brought her up to date. "I have security footage of a car driving by the bar shortly after your father arrived."

"It didn't stop?"

I shook my head. "But it was driving slow as if the person was calculating whether or not to go in."

"Did you get the license plate?"

"I did. But it's a rental. Without suspicion of a crime, I won't be able to get a judge to sign off on a warrant to get more information."

"Will the autopsy help?"

"It could." I was banking on it.

Emma would face backlash if she dug up her father and the medical examiner couldn't label her father's death as either suspicious or a homicide. And unlike wearing my shirt, that was something the town people would never forget.

When they brought up the casket, I held onto her tighter until the contractor came over with something she needed to sign. Then they drove off with her father in a van.

"I don't want to be alone," she said.

The only question was, "Your place or mine?"

"Yours," she said. "I don't care what anyone says."

When we arrived at my place, I had her park her car out back in the garage while I parked my truck in the driveway. No matter what she said, she didn't need the added scrutiny of the town. It would be bad enough when everyone questions why she dug up her father.

Back in my bed, she wore another one of my shirts. This time a favorite baseball tee I'd kept from high school. I hadn't been as big, so this one barely covered her ass.

The sadness in her eyes kept me in check as I held her.

"You can always tell people it's none of their business," I said, after placing a kiss on the top of her head.

"About us or about my dad?" she asked before yawning.

That caught me off guard and I struggled with an answer. Before I could, her breathing evened out. She was tired, and probably not sleeping.

My answer would have to wait.

One thing I did know was staying away from her would be impossible. She felt way too good in my arms to give up without a fight.

SEVENTEEN
EMMA

FOR THE HUNDREDTH time I cursed Jack and one of my other bartenders for calling out sick tonight. Saturdays were the busiest at the bar and I was down two people. It left me with an all-girl crew. It wasn't that I didn't think I could handle it. I was pissed because I was pretty damn sure Jack had done it on purpose to make a point.

It had been a few days since my sleepover at Aiden's. I'd left early without getting spotted. Even my neighbor hadn't caught me slinking into my house around dawn. I hated to leave him, but I didn't want him to get more grief.

Lucky for me, so far no one had been bold enough to ask me about my dad's coffin being dug up. It could have been because a man whose family had all left town passed the day before. People could have assumed they were digging his grave if they saw the dirt and didn't go into the cemetery for a closer inspection.

Josie came over with a drink order. "Emma, I'm sorry to have to put this on you, but that table of guys over there—" she nodded at table eleven.

I knew who she was talking about. I didn't recognize

any of them. They weren't locals. They likely worked on a nearby ranch or with a logging company just out of town. They were drinking heavily and talking way too loudly. I'd been keeping an eye on them worried about trouble.

"What's up?"

She glanced down like she didn't want to tell me. "The one guy with the shoulder length, shaggy hair keeps putting his hands on my ass. I told him politely to stop. Usually—"

"Jack or my dad would have put a stop to it," I finished for her.

She nodded.

"Mind the bar for a minute," I said. I was the only bartender for the night.

Dad kept two things under the bar. A baseball bat and a shotgun. The later was in a hidden gun case that opened by fingerprint. Mine and his were the only ones that could unlock it as far as I knew. That was the one thing he'd invested money in. He'd told me he didn't want to have to use it but wanted it easily accessible if needed. I wasn't even sure Jack knew it was there. It was tucked under a lower shelf. If you bent down and saw it, it looked as if it was part of the structure of the bar, there for support.

I didn't get either and saddled over to the table with a wide smile. I made sure to stop at the corner of the table where said asshole she spoke of sat. "How are you boys doing tonight?" I asked.

All eyes were on my tits, covered as they were, but it didn't matter to them. My tank top was form fitting, and it didn't hide my curves.

"We'd be doing a lot better if you joined us," the asshole said before his hand went right to my ass.

I smiled and leaned down because I wanted to make sure he heard me loud and clear. He took my movement as invitation, grinning like a cat who'd caught a mouse. "If you don't take your hands off me or any of my staff, you'll come to regret it," I said while still smiling before I knocked his hand away not so gently.

The other guys around the table jeered and pointed at him with their peanut gallery comments. It was too bad the asshole's ego was too fragile and he put his hand back. In quick succession, I raised my arm and used my elbow like a battering ram against his nose. Blood squirted and the table got quiet.

"You broke my nose," the asshole whined.

"You're lucky I didn't break your hand, which would put you out of a job. If you want to keep those fingers, keep your goddamn hands to yourself." I didn't curse often, but it felt appropriate here. Then, I sweetly announced to the table, "Don't forget to pay your tab on the way out."

Before I got two feet away, he said, "I should call the cops."

I turned and grinned because his head was tilted back as he held his nose. "Please do because putting your hands on me and my waitresses is called assault and battery." I pointed to his ruined nose. "That's called self-defense. So yes, please call the sheriff so we can put it on the record." When he just sneered at me, I added, "Or maybe you have a record."

By the hate in his eyes, I guessed he did. The kind that had probably had him still on parole and bringing the police would only put his ass back to jail.

"Bitch," he muttered. It was the best he could do.

"Just pay the tab and get the hell out of my bar."

Some of guys who'd played football back when I was in high school came over. Big strapping guys that had been linemen back in the day.

"You need some help, Emma?"

I winced because I really didn't want the asshole to know my name, not that it would have been hard to find out. Still. "I'm fine," I said. "We've come to an understanding. They are leaving right after they pay their bill."

It was important that the town knew I could handle the bar, but that didn't mean I couldn't appreciate four big guys folding their arms over their chests like sentries for the outsiders to do as told. I sashayed away knowing I hadn't made customers for life and didn't care.

"Josie, take them their bill."

She nodded, "Thanks, Emma." Though I'd handled it thoroughly on my own, I could tell she felt better the towns-folk had come to the rescue. I sighed.

When the bar closed, I stood in the door and watched as my staff got in their cars and left. There was no sign of the asshole or his compadres in the parking lot. There was that. I went to Dad's office and closed out the registers. Normally, I would leave a minimal amount in the drawer so it was ready to go the next day. But I had a bad feeling.

Asshole and friends could come back and do damage to the bar. I wouldn't leave them any cash to take with them even though the amount in the registers wouldn't have covered the value of their tab.

When I was finished, I checked the cameras. Again, something I wouldn't normally do. But tonight, the hairs on the back of my neck stood up.

Sure enough, there were now two cars in the parking lot. Asshole stood next to his waiting. His nose wasn't taped up, but it didn't appear to be bleeding anymore.

Instead of dialing dispatch, I called Aiden. It was instinct.

"Emma, is everything okay?"

He sounded half asleep. It was late. "There's trouble at the bar."

I hung up because there wasn't time to explain. I had no idea how long he'd been waiting. He could have been across the street and had watched everyone leave except me. He was shifting on his feet, likely anxious and planning his next move.

His mistake was thinking I was an easy target. My father made sure I wasn't. I could handle myself and like everyone in the state, I was armed.

I checked my gun but left it in my tote bag for easy reach. The thing about guns was if you pointed it at someone, you had to be prepared to shoot to kill. That was how my father taught me. Because I felt confident I could handle him by other means, the gun was a last resort.

After locking up the office, I walked down the hall to the door, checking the camera on my phone as I did. I didn't want to be blindsided. So far, he was still at his car.

One last look at the phone, I dropped it in my bag in favor of my car keys. They were useful weapons in a pinch if you held them right. I opened the back door and made sure he hadn't moved before I stepped out.

"You should leave," I said before he could make any vague threats.

"Why? You're exactly who I'm here to see." His voice came out nasally, which I'd expected given the size of his swollen nose.

"Looking for another lesson on manners?" I asked, taking a few steps toward my car.

"You keep talking and I'll make sure no one thinks you're pretty anymore."

I stilled. "Is that a threat? I want to be clear on what you're doing here."

"Call it whatever you want. But you owe me." His lip curled in an ugly smile that went well with the ugly muddled coloring around his nose.

"Owe you for what?"

"For breaking my nose."

I was careful with my choice of words. "After you assaulted me."

"Whatever bitch. You prance around in your tight clothes because you want a man. A real man, not some small dick city pussy."

Did he know me? I studied his scruffy face, trying to recall who he could be and came up empty. He had a scar on his cheek, but that didn't ring any bells either.

"Last chance. Leave or you'll regret it," I offered.

He chuckled not having learned his lesson earlier. I gave him my back and walked to my car. It was a risk. If his friends were somewhere hidden, I would be in trouble until Aiden or the cavalry arrived.

As I guessed, he was as predictable as he'd been earlier. He did exactly what I wanted him to do. He rushed up behind me and wrapped an arm nearly around my throat. I dropped my bag and grabbed at his arm. Then, I bent, using his momentum to send him over me to land flat on his back.

The air rushed from his lungs, leaving him stunned. I used my boot to pin his hand to the ground as I reached for my gun.

"Stay where you are, or I'll break every finger in your hand like I promised you earlier."

"You bitch," he spat and started to move.

I applied more of my weight on his hand and pointed my gun at his forehead as he stared up at me.

"A bitch with a gun," I said.

Tires screeched, but I couldn't look away or the asshole

122

could get the drop on me. I had to hope the person who'd arrived was Aiden.

"Emma," Aiden said calmly, like he needed to talk me down and maybe he did.

"This bitch is trying to kill me," the asshole cried.

Aiden came into view. His gun was raised, but not pointed at me. "You can put it away."

"Hey stranger," I said. I winked, and I watched Aiden's lips twitch as he tried not to smile. I might have rocked on my feet before I removed my foot from his hand.

The asshole cried out. "Now she's broken my fingers."

I hadn't or at least I didn't think so.

"On your stomach, hands behind your head," Aiden called out.

"What the fuck man? She did this to me."

"I have video and audio of the entire thing," I said, calmly. "He was waiting on me and made threats. When I didn't back down, he came at me. I put him on his ass and his ego is bruised again. I'll send you the video," I offered.

He didn't answer me. He repeated his instructions to the asshole. The sound of Aiden's gun cocking got the asshole moving. He rolled on his stomach and did as asked. Aiden had him in handcuffs in seconds. Then just as fast, he hoisted the asshole up and perp walked him to his SUV.

"That ain't no cop car," the asshole complained.

Aiden flashed his badge and got him in the back passenger side. He used another pair of cuffs to tether him to the headrest. With no barrier, I couldn't blame Aiden.

Then, he came back to me. "What happened?"

I gave him the short version of events. "I may have video of the table incident, but I didn't check. I do have the video of what happened here. And my doorbell will have the audio. We might have been out of view. But there will be audio."

"Send it to me on my office email." He handed me a business card.

"Official."

"Exactly. And go home. Call me when you get there."

"You don't need my statement?"

"Not tonight. The video and audio will be enough for now."

There I went again, wanting to kiss him. I fought against the urge. "Thank you."

"We've talked about this before. You don't have to thank me."

"You were sleeping."

"I was dozing."

I licked my lips. "Thanks anyway." I tore myself from his gaze and went to my car.

"Call me," he said, and I nodded.

Aiden Faulkner would be the death of me if he didn't kiss me soon.

EIGHTEEN
AIDEN

Emma's asshole was all too familiar with me.

"Billy Baker," I said. "Didn't take you long to violate the terms of your parole."

Because there was a restraining order against him by a former girlfriend, the Sheriff's office was notified when he was released from prison.

"That crazy bitch broke my nose and hand."

"She's not a bitch and you know as well as I do you provoked her," I said.

"With words." Spittle flew in my car as he was practically turning purple with rage.

"I doubt that. She's sending me video of the entire thing. You may want to rethink your statement."

"I want a lawyer."

"You'll get one after you're processed."

I pulled into the lot behind the station. Getting him out would be risky. That's why I used two cuffs and not one. Good thing I kept them in my SUV for this very reason. I only had to remove one to release him from the car. If he made a run for it, he would still have his hands cuffed together.

"Don't add to your charges by trying to run," I warned him before I got out.

I braced myself before opening the back passenger door, but he didn't do anything yet. I was vulnerable as I leaned in and released the one cuff. I left it hanging as I hauled him out.

"Maybe I'll tell my lawyer you did this to me, and I'll get off."

I unlocked the back door and so far, he was compliant. I waited until we were inside before I said, "You do remember she has video, which would include me. There's video all over the station," I lied. "The timestamps will prove along with the video that I had nothing to do with your injuries."

"That bitch is lying." He bucked against my hold for the first time.

Wyatt appeared in the hall, and without words exchanged, he helped me get him in the cell.

"I want a lawyer," Billy yelled again.

"After you're processed. Thing about small towns, we don't have overnight personnel to handle things like that. You'll have to wait until the morning."

He yelled at the top of his lungs, and we left the cell area. He was wasting his breath. He would be heading back to jail with no 'pass go' card.

When the door closed, Wyatt finally spoke.

"What the hell happened?"

"Emma called me about trouble at the bar," I said and made my way to my office.

Wyatt trailed me. "Emma called you and not the station?" I shrugged. "So the rumors are true?"

"What rumors?" I asked.

"People have seen the two of you together a lot." He made a point to exaggerate the last two words.

"People are always talking," I said, dismissing it.

"Maybe, but I know you and you've been sweet on her since high school."

Had it been that obvious to everyone? "She's engaged," I said.

"Yeah. She's a sweet girl, Aiden."

"What are you saying?"

"I'm just saying there are rumors about you and Darcy too. And I know how you two are together."

Darcy had come by with floor samples the other day. Apparently, that hadn't gone unnoticed either.

I felt my anger rising. "How's that?"

"You'd be with Darcy one minute and someone else the next. Then Darcy again."

"I didn't cheat on her if that's what you're suggesting. Darcy and I broke up, a lot."

"Exactly. But you'd always end up back with her. Emma's happy. Don't play with her head if you aren't sure."

I leaned back because I was glad someone was looking out for Emma. "There's nothing going on with Darcy and me."

"Someone saw the two of you together in your house. Did they make that up?"

I opened my mouth as it hit me. Darcy had made that move. I thought I'd heard something at the door that night, but then I was holding Darcy off and telling her the score. After Darcy left, I had gone to see Emma and she'd acted so strange.

"They did see something?" Wyatt asked, pulling me out of my thoughts. "I'm just saying. You know how things were with my ex, Karlie. She almost came between Sadie and me. Don't let something like that happen to you."

I checked the time. "I'll be back and when I do, you can go home to your pretty wife. Deal?"

"It's my shift," he said.

"Yeah, and I have paperwork to do. There's no point in both of us being here." I checked my phone. Emma had emailed me the video. I'd send it along with the report later.

"Where are you going?" he asked.

"I'll be back." I wasn't going to answer his question, not with all the rumors going around. I could have waited until the morning. But more eyes would be on me. I pulled to a stop in front of Emma's house. I jogged to the door and knocked. It wasn't hard enough to wake the neighbors, but loud enough to hear.

She came to the door, hair wet.

"You didn't call," I said, though she had emailed me.

"Oh." Her lips curved, and I swear her name carved itself on my heart in that moment.

"Can I come in?"

She tightened her robe and then bobbed her head, taking a step back.

Inside, a large bouquet of red roses was on the kitchen island.

"Are those from Evan?"

She blew out a breath. "Yeah." She didn't sound happy about it.

"An apology or just because?" I asked. I did have my reasons for wanting to know the answer.

"Neither."

"Is it none of my business?" I asked, keeping my eyes on hers.

"I um—broke things off. This is his way of getting me back, I guess."

I held back a satisfactory smile. "You broke the engagement?"

"I did."

"Why?"

We just stared at each other for a long moment.

"It didn't feel right."

I switched gears with purpose. "Why were you mad at me last Friday night?"

"I apologized for that," she said, dodging an answer.

"And I accepted. I'd like to know why you were so angry with me."

She shifted her gaze to the ground. I put a finger under her chin and lifted her head to meet her eyes. "Tell me."

She sighed. "I saw you..."

I didn't force her to finish. I had my answer. "If you'd watched a second longer, you would have seen me setting the record straight with Darcy. There is nothing there for you to be jealous about."

The innocent way she looked at me and then bit her lip, broke me. I leaned down and captured her mouth in a kiss that was a long time in the making.

When she looped her arms around my neck, I walked her back to a wall and pressed into her softness.

My cock responded and I pulled back before she felt the evidence of my arousal. She looked as crestfallen as I felt.

"We have all the time in the world. I'm a patient man and I plan to do this right. When I have you for the first time, there will be no doubt between us as to where we stand. You will belong to me and no other man."

I glanced down at the ring she still wore on her finger despite her claims of breaking up with him.

"I don't belong to him. I wear the ring because it's easier than answering a lot of questions from the busy bodies in town. Evan doesn't want the ring back, but I will give it to him."

I didn't blame her about the gossip. "We can do this your way for now. Slow and steady and out of the prying eyes of the town. Agreed?" A shy smile warmed her mouth as she bobbed her head yes. "I'll talk to you tomorrow."

"You're leaving?" she asked.

"If I stay, it's going to be fast and hard and there's nothing wrong with that," I said. "But I promised slow and steady, which I'm neither at the moment."

Her robe slipped, giving me a naked view of a strip of skin from between her breast down to the tie belted at her waist. It was going to be a long night.

I tipped my head with fingers on the brim of my hat and left. I couldn't risk kissing her again. What I did know that she didn't, was that she was mine. I dared any man, including her ex, to prove me wrong.

And damn if I wouldn't be tested in the very near future.

NINETEEN

EMMA

HAD THAT REALLY JUST HAPPENED? I kissed Aiden Faulkner. Why did I feel like a schoolgirl that needed to call her best friend and share?

"Jessie, I know it's late, but I need to talk to you," I said when she answered. "Promise you won't tell anyone, not even Miles."

"What, that you had your father's body exhumed? When were you going to tell me?"

I sucked in a breath because for a moment, I'd forgotten. "You heard?"

"A few people are wondering. I don't think it's big news yet. Some think the grave is for Old Man Collins." He was the guy that had passed a day before they'd come for my father.

"It's my dad. I'm getting an autopsy."

She was quiet. "I don't know what to say except I'm sorry you had to do that."

"Me too. But I need answers."

"I get it. But that isn't why you called, is it?"

"No." I had to push the sadness back.

"Is it about Aiden?"

"I kissed him, rather he kissed me," I blurted out, hoping to find that joyous moment I had earlier.

"Holy shit."

"Yeah."

"And... how was it?" she asked.

"Everything I hoped and better." Some of the giddiness was back and I tried not to feel guilty about it. "I don't think I've ever been kissed like that before."

I wasn't lying. Kissing Evan had been a chore after the first time. It never felt natural, and I'd assumed it was from my lack of experience. I'd only had a few serious boyfriends.

"Good for you. You deserve it, my friend, and I like Aiden. He was so cute when Janet tried hitting on him. I had to intervene because he was at a loss for words."

"He mentioned that. Not that I blame her."

"Who are you telling? What girl didn't have a crush on Aiden at one point or another while we were in school?"

"Did you?"

"Maybe. A little one. I thought he was hot that's for sure."

We talked a little while longer and then I got off. I needed sleep.

Before I left for work the next day, I had chores to do around the house. Through most of it, I floated. I was certain my feet hadn't touched the ground. Was that what it was supposed to feel like when you were falling in love? Not that I was there with Aiden. But I hadn't ever felt this way with anyone else, including Evan.

By the time I made it to the bar, I couldn't wipe the grin off my face. I didn't even get pissed off when one of my waitresses called out. I put on my apron and got to work.

After the lunch crowd, one of my cooks, Robert

informed me we were low on meat and wouldn't last through the night. I scowled.

"Jack didn't order any?" Though I asked the question, I didn't think he knew the answer.

He shrugged.

"I'm going to run to Sal's and see what I can get." I stormed off having a feeling that Jack was seriously trying to screw me over.

Sal's was behind the police department on a different street, but I could see the back parking lot of the station. I had to pry my eyes away from hoping to catch a glimpse of Aiden.

What was wrong with me? I'd seen him in the middle of the night. The problem was I could still feel his lips on mine.

I got out of my car and went into Sal's.

Sal's niece, Hallie, who was new to town, stood behind the counter.

"Hey, Hallie, it's good to see you." We'd met a few times while getting coffee. "I'm in a jam. I don't think Jack put in my order with Wilder. It seems I'm short on ground beef and won't make it through the dinner hour. Do you have—" I rattled off a number of pounds that made her eyes widen, "I can take off your hands?"

"I'll have to go back and check."

"If you could. I'll take half that, even a quarter could get us through the night. Then, I can straighten things out with Wilder tomorrow."

I swore she blushed. Did she have a thing for Wilder? He was a good-looking guy.

When she came back, she said, "This is what I can get you." She told me the amount and arranged to get it in my car.

It was less than half of what I needed, but beggars couldn't be choosers. "Can you put it on my account?"

She nodded.

"You know we should hang out some time," I said.

"Yeah."

We didn't make exact plans, but now that Jessie had Miles and his adorable son, even I knew we wouldn't be hanging out as much.

I drove back to the bar and made a few trips to haul in the meat with the cook's help. On the last trip, I ran into Jack.

"We need to talk," I snapped.

"Yeah, but I think you need to deal with your boyfriend first. He's asking for you out front."

Evan had been my fiancé, and what I had with Aiden was new. Still, I wasn't sure who he was referring to after all the comments he made about my personal life. I brushed passed him and breezed into the main bar area.

When I spotted Evan talking to Darcy, I didn't miss a step. I found that I had no reaction to their closeness.

"Hey Emma," Darcy said like we were best friends.

I ignored her. "Evan, what are you doing here?"

His carefree expression shifted quickly into a frown. "Is that how you greet your fiancé?"

It didn't matter that we'd gained the attention of everyone in hearing distance. It was time the town knew my relationship status.

"I told you the other day, we aren't together anymore."

He glanced around before flashing me a placid smile. "With everything that's happened, I can understand that you're confused about our future, but I'm not. I'm here because I want us to work."

There wasn't an admission of love, which suited me

fine. I didn't think either of us had really loved one another. I'd cared, not so much anymore, especially after seeing this side of him.

While he'd been going on, I'd worked the ring off my finger. I took his hand and placed it in his palm. "This should clear things up for you. We're done."

"Are you sure?" he asked, his tone turning hostile. "There's no turning back." I let my eyebrow arch in answer. "Fine." He held up the ring. "I don't need this back. It's not like it's real, though no one noticed. Not surprised in this hick town. Though I'd planned to give you a real one once we were married." He set it down on the counter. "Keep it as a reminder of what you've lost." Then he left the bar.

Darcy was on her feet. "Make your choice Emma. You can't have them both. Evan or Aiden. I know who I would choose."

I said nothing. She shrugged and followed Evan. They deserved each other, I thought.

When I spun around, everyone who'd had front seats to the show turned as if minding their own business. I didn't care. I was free. I didn't look at the glass ring, uncaring if anyone took it.

On the way, I pointed to Jack. "My office, now."

For a second, he was startled. I was too. That was the first time I'd claimed Dad's office as mine. As I continued forward, I'd accepted that I'd made up my mind about several things after reading Dad's letter.

"Close the door," I commanded when we went in.

Jack did, albeit a little slowly. "Emma?"

I held up my hand. "You're not my father. I don't need lessons from you on how to run this bar. And don't try to deny it."

He kept his mouth shut.

"Whatever game you think you're playing ends now. And let me tell you, I'm not going anywhere. If you can't work under me, then quit now. But if you stay, you'll treat me with the same respect you treated my father. Your choice."

He stared at me, creating an uncomfortable silence I wasn't willing to give into. I folded my arms instead.

"Are you sure you want to do this?" he asked.

"You know, I'm really tired of being asked that question today. I'm not a little girl." I pulled a copy of Dad's will from under a pile and handed it to him. "Dad left me the bar. He trusted me and you need to as well if you want to continue working here."

He glanced down at the paper and I watched as he scanned the page. When he looked up, I saw the anguish on his face. "This is all I got, Emma. I'm not qualified to do anything else."

That wasn't true. He could go to work for the mill or the ranch if either would have him, but I didn't say that. "Then, you're going to have to work with me, not against me."

He nodded. "Would you consider me being a partner?"

"No. You haven't shown enough respect for me to trust you as a partner." Though I wouldn't commit to anything more, regardless. "I don't want to get your hopes up either. I'm not sure I need a partner."

"Yeah, okay."

I needed more confirmation than that. "Are you in or out?"

"In," he said.

He might have agreed to it, but I could see in his eyes he would likely be making other plans. I would need to hire a new manager soon. Someone I could trust.

After he left, I sagged in my chair, emotionally

exhausted. I glanced down at my naked finger and smiled. I picked up my phone and dialed.

"Emma." My name had never sounded so sweet.

"I have news," I announced.

Damn, his chuckle was sexy. "What's that?"

"My finger is bare and so is my bed."

"Is that an invitation?"

Was it? "I guess you'll have to find out."

TWENTY

AIDEN

WELL, fuck my life. How was I supposed to work after an invitation like that?

I was painfully hard and trying to calm myself down when Bess came in my doorway. "Got a call, Wyatt and Sam are tied up. You're going to need to take it."

Her appearance softened everything that had been hard seconds ago. I had no trouble getting up from my desk and strapping my vest on as Bess explained the who, what, and where of it all.

Ten minutes later, I pulled up in front of a dilapidated house in need of much repair. Bess had warned me what I was walking into, but it was my job to show up regardless.

A woman in her early forties with a cigarette hanging out of her mouth stepped out onto the porch.

"Thank goodness you came. It's smells like something died in there."

From the state of the home's exterior and the abandoned toys overgrown with vegetation, I wouldn't have doubted something had died. Her husband had passed away over two years ago, and she wasn't handling it well.

According to Bess, she called the station every few days about something. Bess speculated the woman wanted company or needed a handyman and couldn't afford one.

When I reached her, she said, "Aiden Faulkner, oh, how you've grown."

I came to a sudden stop as I tried to place her. "You know me?"

She laughed. "I taught you in second grade."

My mind flew back in time. "You were a teacher?" Her name didn't ring any bells.

"I was Miss Wilson back then before I married my good-for-nothing husband, who died and left me with a crumbling house and a pile of bills."

Once she said her maiden name, I remembered the teacher my younger self had a mad crush on. She'd been pretty and nice. The woman before me bore no resemblance to that. Haggard lines etched on her face that had turned the inviting smile I remembered into the bitter scowl she wore today.

"Do you still teach?" I asked.

She shook her head. "My husband didn't want me to."

"He's gone. Maybe you could go back to teaching." It was as if she'd never considered the thought and it wasn't really my place. With no more comments about her life choices, I got back to business. "You called about a smell."

We didn't often go to peoples' homes for smells. But she'd smelled death, which had to be investigated when she'd been unable to pinpoint the culprit.

"It's in here." She waved me in, and I followed her.

The house looked worse on the inside than the outside. It wasn't cluttered, just neglected. Time had taken its toll on the place. But the smell was unmistakable.

I followed her into her kitchen.

"It's in here."

Though I wasn't a bloodhound, I used my nose as I opened cabinets and even drawers looking for the origin of the awful stench. Nothing. "I'm going to check outside," I said.

"I didn't think of that." She opened the back door.

The smell was there too. As I walked alongside the wall, I found it. A rodent had tried to get through a small hole in the wall to the house and had somehow gotten stuck.

"There's your problem," I said, pointing at it.

Her mouth widened before she covered it with one hand and locked her eyes with me. "What can I offer you to help me get rid of that?" she asked, while loosening her robe.

I froze, even though I'd expected as much. Bess had warned me this might happen. Once she revealed she'd taught me as a child, I'd let my guard down.

Years ago, she'd been something to look at. Now she was in her forties but looked a decade or two older. However, that wasn't why I glanced away. Though I would have never used my position to gain such favors, it was an image of Emma in my mind that made it impossible for me to enjoy the view of any other woman.

"If you could get me some gloves, a trash bag and a shovel, I'll take care of it."

Her relief was enough to know I was doing a good deed. Though I would have preferred being at the station going through video footage relating to Emma's dad, my former teacher needed help.

By the time I was done, I'd removed the creature that was causing the stench and plugged the hole it had got stuck in, then fixed her toilet. I managed to leave before she found another thing for me to do off her honey do list.

I was tired, sweaty, and dirty. What did I do? I called Emma.

"Aiden," she said and, man, did I love hearing her say my name.

"Meet me at the creek. You know the spot. That is if you aren't busy."

"I—" She hesitated for a second and said, "Okay. I'll be there shortly."

We hung up.

I could have gone home, showered, and returned to the station. But after her call earlier, I needed to see her badly.

I drove to the hidden cove with a smile the size of Montana on my face. Emma was closer and beat me there. I parked my car on the side of the road near some trees. This stretch of road wasn't widely traveled. In fact, it didn't have a name, just ruts in the ground to mark it.

"Why are we here?" she asked, all grins and giggles.

"Let's see, I just finished playing handyman for my old teacher, Miss Wilson, and need to wash the smell of dead rodent off my skin."

"And you thought of me? I'm flattered."

I eyed her bare finger. "I thought of you for plenty of reasons. For one, school is still in session, so we'll have this place to ourselves."

"It's cold," she mentioned, faking a shiver when she wore short sleeves.

"I'm hoping you'll warm me up."

She tapped a finger on her lips. "I'm to warm you up?"

"Yes," I said, taking a step closer to her.

"And what about me?"

"I'll keep you warm too." I was closing the distance between us.

I caught the twinkle in her eye a second too late as she

took off. Damn she could run. By the time I reached the short cliff over the water's edge, she was halfway out of her clothes. I could have nabbed her then, but I wanted her to shed her jeans.

Just as I had mine halfway down my calves, she leaped off and splashed into the water. I was right there after her, cannonballing my way in.

Water cocooned me for the moment. In that split second, all the memories of coming out here with friends struck me. Emma would have been here too on occasion. Though off to the side. She hadn't been a flashy girl like Darcy who wanted the attention. But I'd caught her looking my way a time or two, and she had to have caught me staring or so I assumed. I broke the surface with a thought.

"What took you so long, stranger," she teased.

I swam over to her. "I was just thinking," I began.

"About what?"

"About how much I wanted you back in high school."

She looped her arm around my neck. "Why didn't you have me?"

I groaned. "By the time you grew up, I was in a complicated relationship."

"Complicated, huh?"

"Very complicated. Besides, you had boyfriends too if I remember."

"I did. Though none of them compared to this."

Her gaze was equally locked on me as I said, "Maybe it was better we didn't have *then*."

"Why?" she asked, scrutinizing me with a look.

"Because I probably would have made mistakes, young and dumb as I was."

"Pussy-whipped by Darcy," she suggested.

"Maybe a little of that and a lot of guilt," I said. Darcy

143

had been good at using her tears until I became immune to them.

"Now that you have me, what are you going to do about it?"

I didn't answer with words. I showed her. I promised slow and steady, so I didn't rush the kiss. My movements weren't hurried as I licked across the seam of her lips until she gasped. Then, I dipped in and did a little slow dance with my tongue against hers.

We waded over to a spot where my feet touched bottom, yet we were mostly submerged. She wrapped her legs around me and I held her tight.

"I've waited for this so long," she said.

"Me too."

Her core was perfectly placed on the ridge of my hard cock. Nothing but a shift of my boxers down and her underwear to the side, and I could be inside her in under a minute. As much as I wanted to fuck her raw, I didn't act.

She rocked her hips against me almost breaking my resolve. We would fuck. "Not here," I said, on a long exhale of breath.

She sighed too.

Her little moans and writhing against me forced my hand. Rather, I gave in to giving her the pleasure she sought but with my fingers, leaving my cock hard and jealous. I worked her tight bundle of nerves before slipping one, then two fingers inside her heat while thrusting until she found her release. I kept kissing her until we were both breathless.

When the water had calmed around us, no longer rippling from our movements, she said, "Aren't you supposed to be working?"

God, she was sexy, and it was taking all my resolve to wait this out. I had to remind myself she was so worth the wait. "I am actually. I think I have a lead on your father's case." That had been my other motivation to see her.

"What?" she asked. There was a fierce woman inside her. Determination was beating out sadness.

"I told you about the video from the auto body?"

"Yes," she said.

"I was caught up trying to watch the car that went by slowly. After I went forward, it shows your father leave."

"He left?"

"Yes, he was at the bar maybe twenty minutes and then he left."

"Where did he go?" she asked, but I didn't think she expected me to answer.

"I couldn't see from that angle, but he came back maybe fifteen minutes later, and he wasn't alone."

Her eyes grew. "You know who it was?"

"Unfortunately, no. The problem was, I never saw them leave."

I'd been watching over and over again, hours before her father came and hours after. The angle was off. It was possible they could have left another way. "We're getting close," I said, feeling it in my gut. I could go canvas the town for more video, but the autopsy had begun. If I waited, I should have what I needed for a formal investigation.

"There's something you should know," she said, untangling herself from me. She waded away, putting space between us, and I didn't like it.

"Evan came to the bar today and he wasn't alone."

"This is when you gave the ring back to him?"

She grinned. "Oh, it should be news in town. Least of which was that he admitted to me the ring didn't have a real diamond."

"Asshole."

"No, it's fine. Honestly, I felt better. I thought I was hurting him when I wasn't. He didn't love me. He loved the idea of me. The native backwater girl whom he could show the world through his prism. My dad had been right about him all along."

"I'm still, sorry. You deserve better."

She shrugged. "A learning experience. Besides, I have you."

I swam in closer and kissed her because I couldn't stop.

She grinned and held up a finger. "You'll want to know this. The interesting thing is Darcy acted like she knew him."

"Okay," I didn't see where she was going until I did.

"Like she really knew him. She dared me to choose between the two of you as if she'd be happy to take the other."

Though I shouldn't be shocked, I was, somewhat. "Darcy told me she had a thing with the mayor."

Emma gave me a look like I was dense. "The mayor's too full of himself to settle down. I don't know. But Darcy seemed a little too sure of herself."

Would Darcy sleep with Emma's fiancé? I wanted to think no, but that wouldn't be what any other investigator would consider if they didn't have a close relationship with her. It was time I had a talk with Darcy.

"I've got to get to the bar," Emma said. "Jack and I have come to an understanding, but I don't know how long it will last. I'll see you later," she said.

We got out of the water and used towels I had in the back of my car. I was prepared for almost every situation, including a change of clothes.

"Will I see you tonight?" I asked.

When she looked at me like she did now, I lost my breath every time.

"I'll be late," she said.

"My door will be unlocked."

She grinned.

I watched her drive away. Emma Hawkins was mine and she'd be my wife, even if she didn't know it yet.

TWENTY-ONE
EMMA

IT WAS HARD LEAVING AIDEN. A part of me had wanted to cross that finish line right there in the cove. We'd been alone, I'd been reasonably sure of that. The other part was scared. What if I didn't live up to his expectations? It wasn't like I had the kind of carnal knowledge about sex that Darcy did.

Though I'd told Aiden I had to go to the bar, I needed a shower after that. Only, there was a car parked in front of my house. It wasn't close to my neighbors. Whomever it was, wanted to see me.

I got out knowing that the out of state license plate could only be one person.

"Were you with him?" Evan's car door had opened the minute my feet hit the pavement. "Have you been screwing him this entire time?"

I didn't want to have this conversation especially out on the street. No doubt, my neighbor, Ms. Watson, was watching from her window. But I also didn't want him inside my house. I didn't like the hate beaming from his eyes.

"What does it matter? You've been screwing Darcy." Though I'd angrily threw that at him, I honestly didn't care if he had.

"If you'd pry your legs open more than just occasionally, I wouldn't have to fill my needs elsewhere."

There were so many things I could say, like if he'd been good in bed, he wouldn't have to pry my legs open. But I was done with the conversation.

"No worries now. You're free to screw whoever you want." I left him standing on the street or at least I tried.

He caught up to me and wrenched my arm so that I spun to face him.

"I've invested a lot in you," he sneered.

"Yeah, like what the ring cost you? Twenty-five cents from the gum ball machine." I tried to yank my arm away. He gripped tighter, pulling me closer.

"You won't make a fool of me. We're getting married."

Pain hurdled through my arm where his hold felt like the Jaws of Life had clamped down on me.

"Let me go," I seethed through gritted teeth.

"You belong to me," he said, his other hand grabbing my ass.

Sirens resonated in the distance. I glanced over to see the curtain move in my neighbor's window. A Sheriff's SUV came barreling down the lot. Evan was so surprised he hadn't released me.

Aiden came around his vehicle which he'd parked to the side of us. He glanced at me and then narrowed his eyes at Evan.

"Release her," he said, using a commanding voice. Though he appeared calm, there was a storm brewing behind his eyes.

"Officer, there's not a problem. I'm with my fiancée,

right Emma?" Evan had the nerve to think I'd agree with him.

I jerked, but his hold was firm. "It's actually Chief Deputy Sheriff and I got a call about a disturbance. Ms. Hawkins, are you okay?"

Though I let him see it in my eyes, I said, "No. He won't let me go."

Aiden's hand slipped to the butt of his gun. "Sir, I'm going to ask you again to release her."

"Fine," Evan barked and pushed me away.

I hadn't been expecting it and my heel caught the edge of the curb and I went down, hard on my butt. I didn't see what happened next only that Evan was wrestled to the ground, his arms wrenched behind his back.

"You have the right to remain silent," Aiden began to recite the Miranda warning I'd heard so many times on TV shows as he heaved him to his feet and perp walked him back to his vehicle.

"You broke my nose, you asshole. I'm going to sue you," Evan screamed as Aiden shut him in the back of his vehicle.

Then, he was there beside me. The situation was almost déjà vu to that of the guy I'd had to teach a lesson to at the bar. Too bad the town hadn't seen that. "Are you okay?"

I nodded. "I hadn't expected it. He caught me off guard." Evan had never showed this side of himself to me. We'd had verbal fights, all couples did. It had never gotten physical. "Can you arrest him?"

Aiden grinned. "He assaulted you."

"I don't know that I want to press charges," I said without thinking.

"You don't have to. I witnessed it, along with your neighbor. Besides, maybe the fear of prosecution will make him leave you alone." His eyes dropped to my wrist, which was ringed in a red handprint. "You should go let the doc check you out."

I murmured an agreement as I caught a side view of Evan spitting mad in the back of Aiden's SUV. His eyes were wild, and it scared me. "Are you sure you're okay? I can call Jessie for you."

"I'm fine. I'll call her."

He looked like he wanted to kiss me, but he didn't. "I'll call you later." I nodded, and he marched around to his driver's side door all cop-like. I didn't want him to go. I could handle myself in a fight, but Evan rattled me simply because I'd never expected it. My mind drifted to a not so long ago future that might have been mine. What if I'd married him and he'd gotten violent? It had come out of nowhere. I shook myself out of that because that future had been thwarted, gratefully. At least I knew now what he was capable of.

As I walked to my house, I waved at my neighbor. Her nosiness had come in handy. I'd been gearing up to use some of my self-defense training. I'd also been so confused that Evan the monster had been the same man I'd been engaged to. That was part of the reason I hadn't reacted quicker.

Under the shower, I allowed myself a little weakness and cried. Cried because I hadn't listened to my father, who'd seen something about Evan he didn't like. I'd assumed he believed no one would be perfect for me because he'd never liked any of my boyfriends.

I folded my arms and propped them against the tiles, resting my head on them. "I miss you," I said out loud, hoping my father heard me. When would the pain ease? I had no one to ask. Aiden had both of his parents and so did Jessie.

Though I'd been there before when Mom died, I had my dad to lean on. He could have buried himself in his own grief, but he'd been there for me. He'd shown me the light when I'd believed it was my fault. She'd only gone out because of me.

What I hadn't told anyone was that I also felt responsible for Dad's death. We'd had a fight over Evan. Dad and I didn't fight often and when we did, it was never anything monumental. It would be over and done before we could think too hard about it.

That last night had been different. I'd wanted my father's approval so badly when he didn't give it, I'd lashed out. And now he was gone, and I could never take back my words or tell him he was right. I couldn't tell him how much I loved and respected him.

The evidence of how stupid I'd been was the bruise on my arm. Out of the shower, I decided not to go to the docs. My arm hurt, but nothing ibuprofen couldn't take care of.

I fished out a cuff bracelet. It was wide enough to hide the marks. I thought about the women that covered up evidence of abuse and convinced myself this was different. I wasn't doing it to protect him. I was doing it to avoid questions and then the answers I would have to give.

Then I left, locking up my house tight and wishing I had a better security system like the one I had at the bar. I had no idea how Evan was going to react to being locked up. I didn't think I knew the real person who'd hidden behind a mask our entire relationship.

I hated the shaky feeling that consumed me on the way to the bar. I forced myself to walk on steady feet as I kept an eye on my surroundings. Sure, it was prudent for anyone to do that. I didn't like doing it here or at home where I'd spent my life feeling safe.

I planted myself in my office but didn't shut the door all the way. Jack barged in minutes later with fury reddening his face. "Let me see," he demanded, as Jessie barreled into the room after him.

The office seemed smaller with two additional people hovering over my desk. Jack had my arm in his hand, and I sighed before removing the cuff.

"Holy shit," Jessie exclaimed.

"I'll kill him," Jack muttered.

"You'll do no such thing. He's locked up anyway."

"I'll slash his tires," Jessie promised.

"You won't do that either. The last thing I want is his car at my house any longer than need be."

"Miles is on his way over," Jessie said.

"You didn't?" I asked her with a glare.

"I did," she said, holding my gaze as if daring me to say something else.

"Does everyone know?" I said, throwing up my hands.

"Most do," Jessie said.

"You should go home," Jack said. "I'll handle things here today."

I held his gaze. "It's a bruise. I hardly think it will affect me running numbers."

Jessie got a text from Miles. "I'm going to bring him back." She left the office.

"I know you don't want to hear this, but with your father gone, he would want me looking out for you."

"I'm fine," I snapped, but then took a deep breath. "I appreciate you wanting to help, but really I'm fine."

He nodded. "Okay then. I'll get back to work."

After he left, I put my head in my hands, only for Miles to be hustled over by Jessie. "See," she pointed.

I gave in and let him exam my arm. He even took

pictures. "You might want a record of this someday. Maybe not now, but if you do in the future, you'll have it."

Of course, Jessie thought it was funny to photo bomb a few of the pictures. I loved her more for trying to make me feel better.

When they left, I shut and locked the door. I was more out of sorts than I'd admitted, but too spooked to go home.

Aiden texted me later that he would be late. He told me where he kept a spare key and for me to use it.

I did.

In his room, I took off my clothes and got a shirt from his drawer before I slipped between his sheets. His pillow smelled faintly of him as I buried my face in it. Being that close to him even when he wasn't there was the balm I needed to drift off into sleep.

Somewhere in the night, I felt him gather me in his arms.

I might have heard him say, *this is where you belong. Right here with me.* Or had I imagined that?

TWENTY-TWO

AIDEN

EMMA'S EX-FIANCÉ was a piece of work. I'd had to tune out his lunatic ravings on the way to the station so I wouldn't do anything stupid.

As it stood, I deserved an award for not going all bad cop on him when I saw his hands on her. He fought me arresting him, and he didn't disappoint by fighting me into the station. It was déjà vu all over again. Billy 2.0.

"I want my lawyer," he hollered as I put him into one of the cells. "And I'm going to sue your ass."

The door closed and I sighed. As much as I wanted to beat the crap out of him, I couldn't. That wasn't my job.

I went to the front to tell Bess I'd brought in the guy causing the disturbance. After leaving Emma, I'd almost made it back to the station when Bess radioed in that Ms. Watson, Emma's neighbor had called about trouble in front of Emma's house. I turned on my lights and sirens which wasn't necessary most of the time here in Mason Creek and high-tailed it over there.

Emma wasn't a weeping willow of a woman. She hadn't been as a girl either. How she'd handled Billy was proof of that. To see the fear in her eyes when I rolled up had stirred something primal in me. I wanted to get out of the car, guns blazing. Evan was the kind of guy to exploit that. I'd done my job by the book. I didn't smash his head in the ground even when I wanted to.

I balled my hands in fists wishing for the time of gunslinger punishment or even a good fight.

Wyatt wasn't in, so I found Sam. "I need you to handle the asshole in the cell back there."

Evan was the only prisoner at the moment. So, I didn't need to give further information about who.

"Let him call his lawyer in," I checked my watch, "two hours. If he puts up too much of a stink, then an hour. I don't want him out tonight." I wanted to be with Emma when he got out.

"What are we charging him with?" Sam asked.

"Assault, assaulting an officer, resisting arrest. That should do it for now."

Sam nodded and left while I did the paperwork. Evan ranted the entire time. I wondered if he would have a voice by the time his lawyer showed up.

I'd wanted to talk to Darcy, but that would have to wait. I didn't want to leave Sam or Bess to deal with the asshole. They weren't used to his type. I'd worked in LA, and I knew guys like him all too well. A guy who thinks his self-importance was tied to their bank account and used bullying to get what they wanted. He couldn't intimidate me. So, I stayed.

Hours later, a man in a crisp suit walked in. It was late and Bess was gone. I heard the bell and greeted the man.

"Can I help you?" I asked.

"I'm here to pay whatever bail to get Evan Daily out of jail."

I made a show of checking my watch. "That will have to wait until the morning. Everyone is gone for the evening."

"I'd like to talk to my client," he said.

I showed him to the back where the cells were and grabbed him a chair in case he wanted to sit in front of the bars. Then, I left them.

Twenty minutes later, I heard a knock on the cell area door, and I went to open it.

"Can we talk?" the lawyer said.

I took him to my cramped office as there weren't many places to have private conversations at the station. We didn't have the crime that warranted conference rooms and multiple interrogation rooms. We did have one of the later, but it was smaller than my office and didn't seem appropriate for this meeting.

After he sat, I did. He didn't wait for me to speak.

"It seems my client's rights were violated when he was arrested. I think the best thing for you to do is to release him and I'll get him not to sue the department."

I put my hands behind my head and leaned back. "Really? You probably think a small department like this doesn't have updated technology, but we do. We have video cameras on our cars and body cameras." I sat up and pulled mine from the drawer. Not everyone in the department used it. But it was here, and I was used to using it in LA. "I can show you the footage of your client holding a woman against her will. I had to ask him twice to release her. When he did, he shoved her to the ground. While arresting him, he fought me. And you know what else? I've found out this isn't the first time your client has assaulted someone."

"That was dismissed," the lawyer said.

I arched a brow. "Only because it was settled out of

court. Maybe if you let him pay for his crimes, he wouldn't be an asshole."

He wasn't deterred. "What can we do to fix this?"

"Like I said, he needs to pay for his crimes and learn a lesson that there are consequences for his actions. But believe me, I will suggest to the victim that she pursue a civil case against him. There are pictures of the bruises he inflicted that match with the video, you see." The lawyer looked grim. "Anyway, you can see if he's granted bail in the morning."

"Is there somewhere to stay?"

I grinned. "There is a motel out on the highway, five or so miles south of here." There was a better one north, but he didn't ask me for better, did he? I showed him out and left Sam in charge with instructions to ignore the prisoner unless he needed medical attention.

I reached out to Darcy and she texted me her apartment number and asked me to come over.

The apartment complex she lived in was near the covered bridge. I'd never been inside until now.

After a quick knock, she tore open the door and threw herself in my arms.

"Oh, Aiden," she cried.

Darcy was strategic when she cried. However, when I pulled back to read her expression, I noticed the bruise.

"Did he hit you?"

She bobbed her head.

"Tell me what happened," I asked because I didn't want to be an ass and ask her who hit her. I assumed it was Evan.

"He was all pissed off that Emma had embarrassed him at the bar." So, it was Evan. "He came here, and I tried to calm him down. I might have suggested she'd moved on with one of the cops in town." When I narrowed my eyes, she said, "I didn't tell him who. Anyway, he blew up, slapped me, and called me a liar. I told him to get out."

"Did he?" I said, feeling a fresh wave of anger. I may not be in love with Darcy, but we'd spent too many years together for me not to care about her.

"Yeah. I was never more grateful for bolt locks."

"What time was that?"

She told me.

"He went for Emma after." The timeline fit.

"What? Did he hurt her?"

I nodded. "He's in jail for now, but I suggest you not talk to him or open the door for him if he comes back. Do you want to press charges?"

"I don't know."

I didn't like that look in her eyes. "I can't tell you what to do, but if no one speaks up, he won't stop." I hated guilt tripping her, but that was the truth. I saw it far too often in LA. Battered women taking their abuser back. The vicious cycle usually ended up with someone's death. Most of the time it was the victim.

"What should I do if he comes back?" she asked.

"Call me," I said, before I could think. "Better yet, call the station or 911 so it's on the record."

"Will you keep me safe?" she asked.

"I won't let anything happen to you," I promised and shouldn't have. Even I knew, if it came to a choice, I would choose to save Emma over her.

She threw herself at me again. I caught her and sighed as she shook from tears.

"No one's ever hit me before. Not even my daddy."

I got her a bag of ice and ibuprofen and told her to rest before I left. I longed to be home and comforting Emma. I felt guilty that I was here.

Before I left, I remembered why I'd come. "Darcy."

"Mm, hmm," she said, curled on her couch.

"How long have you been seeing Evan?"

"It was only one time a few weeks ago, I think. He'd been flirting with me all week, and then he called and said he couldn't stop thinking about me. I fell for it. It was late and I was lonely."

"Do you think you could pinpoint what day that was?"

She sighed. "Probably. I'll check my phone later and text you. Is that okay?"

I nodded and left. I would have gone home, but I got a call to respond to another domestic event on the other side of town. Two brothers. One woman. It had turned ugly. Wyatt had responded but called for backup.

That one took a while. It was late when I finally arrived home. I stood in the doorway for a while just watching Emma sleeping in my bed.

It made my hellish day turn into heaven sliding in next to her. She was warm, soft, and mine.

"This is exactly where you belong," I whispered in her hair as she circled into me. "Right here with me."

I'd slept next to enough women to know the difference.

TWENTY-THREE

EMMA

SUNSHINE on my skin drew me out of my dreams. It wasn't the sun that warmed me but Aiden's body cocooned around me, heating not only my skin but every inch underneath. If I didn't leave his bed now, I couldn't be blamed for what I would do next.

I slipped quietly out of bed and went for a run. I didn't care who spotted me. Let the town talk; I knew what I was doing. That was all that mattered.

Running in the morning was to me the equivalence of drinking coffee. The fresh air and working my muscles cleared my thoughts.

With every step, I worked through the anger and fear I'd felt. I hadn't reacted well in the face of Evan's hostility. Never again. If he came at me, he would need either heaven or hell to save him if he tried to hurt me again. I smiled at my resolve, feeling better. I circled back and found I enjoyed the view of the mountains in the morning. Dad and I had hiked there many times over the years.

My steps faltered when I was almost back to Aiden's

house. What would Dad think of me? How would he feel about my budding relationship with Aiden?

I didn't have to think too hard about the answer. The words in his letter replayed in my mind. He trusted me to make the right decision.

When I walked in, Aiden was downstairs in the kitchen. "Morning stranger." He winked. "Coffee?"

Damn him for being so darn sexy. "Soon. I'll have water first," I said, and ran a hand over his hair before kissing his cheek.

He grinned and moved to the refrigerator and took out a bottle of water, handing it to me. He then opened a cabinet and grabbed two mugs. I found myself memorizing where to find things.

"Any plans today?" he asked, having caught me watching him.

"Funny enough, yeah." A notification had popped up on my phone. "I scheduled a haircut over a month ago." I laughed at the startled look on his face. "It's just a trim."

"It's your hair. No matter what, I'll still find you the most beautiful woman in the world."

I pursed my lips in good humor. "I bet you say that to all the girls," I teased.

"You'd be wrong. I've only ever said that to you."

The water not only cooled my throat, but it also helped keep the fire that raged inside me. "What are we doing here?" I asked. My heart was getting tangled up in him, and I needed to know where his head was at.

He stopped and turned to face me. He leaned back on the counter as I found the wall at my back. Several feet separated us, but there was an electricity that crackled between us.

"That's all up to you," he said.

"I feel like I've liked you my whole life," I admitted.

"Same here."

"I'm afraid." When he said nothing and didn't look like he'd breathed, I added, "I'm afraid if things don't work out between us, I'll lose an important friend."

"I'll be honest and say I don't want to be your friend, Emma. I've waited most of my life not to be your friend."

"So what do we do?" I whispered.

"Take things slow, very slow."

I nodded, but I kept the honesty going. "I don't think I can keep sleeping in your bed and not want you inside me."

His eyes either darkened or dilated. Whatever it was, the intensity of it pinned me. The flutter of butterfly wings vibrated in my belly.

"You can't say things like that and expect me to keep things slow," Aiden said.

"I don't want to ruin things." Evan's words about my lacking in bed, as much as I'd pretended to discard them, had stung. If I went there with Aiden, would he find me lacking too? It was part of the reason why after Aiden had gotten me off at the cove, I'd run afterwards.

"Me either." He pushed off and stalked over to me. His calloused hand cupped my cheek before he bent down and placed a tentative kiss on my mouth.

He pulled back and I bit my lip before saying, "I should go. I have an early appointment."

"Wait." He checked the time and held up a finger. He took out his phone, pressed a few buttons and put it to his ear. "Has our guest left?" he asked the person on the other line. I couldn't hear the response, but he nodded. "Okay, thanks Bess." When he got off, he said, "Evan's not out yet. I'd like to follow you to your appointment before heading to the station. But I need to grab a shower first if you have time."

"I was actually going to go home first to do the same."

He kissed me again. "I like you in my bed."

"I like waking in your bed."

"You really need a change of clothes and other things here, so you don't have to go home in the morning." His gaze burned into me.

"I thought you said slow." My checks were a raging inferno as I felt his arousal against me.

"This is slow. Otherwise, I'd pick you up, put you on the counter and screw all the rules I've given myself when it comes to you."

"What rules are those?" I asked, feeling far from shy.

"To take my time. We have forever in the making."

"And what if I don't want to wait." That truth warred with the fear of losing him.

"I'd remind you that you've just broken up with your fiancé. I don't want to be your rebound. There's a lot going on in your life right now. I will be patient if it gets me the forever I want with you."

"How can you know that?"

"Because the grass was never as green as it is in your yard. I've loved you from afar for as long as I can remember."

"Why did you wait?" I asked.

"Advice from someone important."

"Are you going to tell me that advice?"

"One day, not today," he said.

"Then, I suggest you go grab that shower because I'm not feeling very patient."

He placed another heart-stopping kiss on my lips. "I promise I'm worth the wait," he said, cheekily.

I hope I am, I thought as he jogged upstairs. I finished my bottle of water and went for the coffee. I could have changed out of Aiden's shirt, but I didn't. I was upstairs in his room gathering my things when he came out of the shower.

Neither of us spoke. He moved to his dresser, grabbed clothes, placed them on his bed before dropping the towel. My mouth could have caught flies as it hung open. Aiden just watched me watching all of him, as he got dressed.

"You're not playing fair," I managed in a choked whisper.

His mouth curled up on one side in a smirk that could make any woman self-destruct. "Let's go," he said once his uniform shirt was buttoned.

All I could imagine was his long thick cock that hung between his thighs a second ago. It took me that long to get my feet moving. I thought about the bundle of clothes in my hands and how he'd suggested I leave some things here. I'd never lived with anyone except my father and had no idea how the dating thing where you stayed at each other's places and left things behind worked. I'd have to ask some of my more knowledgeable friends.

My thoughts sobered when I came to a stop in front of my house. Evan's car was still there. I glared at it. I wouldn't allow him to make me afraid. I practically slammed the car door as I got out and stomped to my front door before Aiden caught up.

"He's never going to touch you again."

His pronouncement thawed some of my fury. I reached up and almost touched his hair. It was still damp, and I almost kissed him before remembering my nosy neighbor. A glance at her house didn't reveal her ever present vigilance at watching over the neighborhood. Still, I unlocked the door and let Aiden inside.

"Go get your shower," he said.

I dumped my purse on a side table and left my shirt there as well. As I ascended the stairs, I took off his shirt and let it fall. Then, my jeans.

"Emma." It sounded more like a growl than a word.

"Two can play…"

I tossed my bra downstairs and then my underwear when I reached the top. I walked straight to the bathroom. Part of me wanted him to chase me. Then, we could end the stalemate. If he thought me lacking in bed, then I could find out sooner before my heart was too tangled in his.

He didn't come. I stayed far too long under the shower, and I'd likely be late for my appointment if I didn't get a move on. Reluctantly, I left the bathroom. Aiden wasn't in my bedroom, and the house was silent. Had he left?

I got dressed and went downstairs. My clothes were gone from the stairs and landing. He'd folded them and set them on top of the shirt I'd left on the side table. His shirt was still in the pile.

Was he leaving his things here too? A little thrill zipped through me.

I went out onto the front porch and joined Aiden who wore a grim expression. I looked out onto the street. Evan's car was gone.

"What happened?" I asked.

"I'll tell you later. You're going to be late."

He followed me to the salon but didn't get out. After I parked, I jogged over to his car.

"Thanks for everything," I said.

"One day, you're going to stop thanking me and just

accept I'm here for you." My eyes dropped to his lips. "Your choice," he said, and he didn't have to tell me what.

I could kiss him and let the town know we were a thing, or I could wait. I leaned in and kissed him. It wasn't long, but when I pulled back there was a big smile on his face.

"My girl has kissed me. I wonder how long before someone asks me about it?"

Though I'd gotten a little thrill by him calling me his girl, I glanced around. "I don't think anyone saw."

"Maybe not, but now I can kiss you when I want."

I sauntered away and went into the salon. "Hey, Faith," I said, my cheeks felt as red as a cherry tomato.

"Hey you," she said. "So, it's true. You and the chief deputy sheriff are a thing?" I shrugged. "It's a good thing." Her eyes dropped to my arm where I'd forgotten the cuff to hide the bruise Evan had given me. "Aiden's one of the good ones. A trim?" she asked.

"I think he likes my hair as is."

Faith laughed. "Yeah, probably better to do something drastic after you walk down the aisle," she joked.

I laughed. "I do have a question."

"Go ahead. Judgment free zone here."

"What are the kinds of things you can leave at a boyfriend's house and what's too much?"

"Good thing we have a little time," she began and schooled me on the etiquette of dating.

TWENTY-FOUR

AIDEN

It had taken a Herculean effort not to follow Emma up those stairs and give into the desire we both felt. I'd been truthful with her when I said I wanted more. If that meant waiting until I was sure she was ready, I'd wait.

To keep me sane, I stepped outside. Hearing the shower running wouldn't help my mental fortitude. Instead, my brain shifted gears. Doug Hawkins's killer, who was he or even a she?

Frustration broiled over as I felt powerless to help Emma find the person responsible. My hands were tied even with the leads I had because all led nowhere without more information. I couldn't get that information without some proof that a crime was committed. It was a catch-22 situation. Hopefully, the autopsy would give us the proof I needed to open a formal investigation where I could get the judge to sign off on warrants to gain me the information I needed.

Jack was still high on my list. I couldn't ask him for an alibi yet, not legally at least.

I checked my phone. Darcy hadn't texted me the information I requested yet. Just as I put my phone back in my pocket, a car drove down the lane. There were only a few houses on this street and the car didn't slow, so they had to be headed here. Evan. I stood straighter. He wouldn't make a scene or upset Emma.

Since the road ended just past Emma's house, the car circled back at the end before pulling to a stop beside Evan's vehicle.

A window rolled down. "Morning, officer," Evan's tidy lawyer said. "I hope we will have no problem here."

"As long as your client doesn't start any," I called from the porch.

The lawyer turned his head and said something to Evan. The passenger's door opened, and he climbed out. I thought of Emma and Darcy and how this man had manhandled them both. I gripped the railing tighter to ensure I didn't break the laws I'd sworn to uphold.

Evan didn't speak, likely based on the advice of his lawyer. His glare however said everything he didn't. I maintained a bored expression because he didn't scare me. I'd been in enough scrapes over the years to trust my abilities. It was a time like this where I wished I didn't wear the shield. A good old fashion kick in the ass would do the pompous bastard good.

As he reached his car, he finally spoke. "Emma's never going to stay in this town for you. And when she's gone..." He got into his car and turned it on before I could react. He whipped it around to the other side and sped off.

"You should remind your client of the speed limit laws here in town. I'd hate to have to pull him over on a misdemeanor charge. It wouldn't go well with his current list of charges," I said to his lawyer.

In response, the man rolled up his window and drove

off. However, I did see him putting his phone to his ear. Unfortunately, Montana didn't have distracting driving laws, so I couldn't do anything about the lawyer talking on his phone while driving. Too bad. I really wanted to make my day brighter by writing them both citations.

Not long after, the door opened behind me. Emma asked me what was wrong. I put off the conversation until later. Instead, I followed her to the salon.

I thought she'd park and go in for her appointment, but she surprised me by coming to my vehicle instead.

As she talked, I listened, yet wondered when we wouldn't hide our feelings for each other in front of the town.

When her eyes dropped to my lips, I said, "Your choice." I was playing by her rules though I was determined to win.

She leaned in and I met her halfway. The softness of her lips wasn't lost on me as I was fully aware of every touch that passed between us. She pulled back far too quickly for my liking. Yet, she'd crossed the first barrier we'd been dancing around for weeks.

"My girl has kissed me. I wonder how long before someone asks me about it?" I joked.

It was cute how she nervously glanced around. "I don't think anyone saw."

"Maybe not, but now I can kiss you when I want." It was a promise I hoped she understood.

Then she was walking away, leaving me mesmerized by the sway of her hips. I waited until she was behind the closed door before driving to the station with a smile on my face.

Darcy's text came as I'd entered through the back and

heard yelling from the sheriff's office. I went past the closed door to see Bess first.

"What the hell is going on here?" That had been clearly heard by anyone in the station.

Bess gave me a sympathetic look before saying, "Sheriff's back and he's looking for you."

I sighed and headed back in that direction. I knocked on the door.

"Is that you, Aiden?" he asked through the door.

"Yes, sir."

"Get in here," he bellowed. I pushed the door open as he hung up his desk phone. He gestured with his hand for me close the door. Once it was, he laid into me. "Do you want to tell me why Doug Hawkins grave was dug up?"

I didn't flinch. "To determine cause of death, sir."

He narrowed his eyes at me. "He died due to a heart attack."

"The evidence suggests something else."

"What evidence?" he barked.

I laid it out for him from the missing surveillance video to the videos I'd gotten from the jewelry story and auto body shop.

"That's not enough to open an investigation," Sheriff said with a scowl.

"Not after the fact, no. But couple that with the autopsy and we will have what we need."

"And when the result comes back saying he died of natural causes, then what? You've given Emma hope where there's none."

"Respectfully, sir, you gave her platitudes. There was enough to rule the death as suspicious when he was found. If you'd done even a little investigation, you would know he wasn't alone when he died. That was enough to open an investigation."

"Who was he with?"

"That's what I intend on figuring out. Give me the go ahead to investigate and I'll find out."

He studied me. I was certain he wanted to tell me to move on, but he couldn't, not anymore. "You don't have enough to get a judge to sign off on anything."

"Only because the death certificate says natural causes."

He pursed his lips. "This isn't LA," he ground out.

"That doesn't mean there aren't bad people. I know you don't want to think anyone is town is capable of murder. That shouldn't stop justice being served."

"You do nothing until those autopsy results are in and stay away from Evan. He's made a formal complaint about you."

I gave him a curt nod. "I have my dash and body cams to show I followed procedure," I said.

Though I had no intentions of not following up on leads where I could. Especially as I decided what to do with the new information Darcy had given me.

"Dismissed," he said.

When I left his office, I headed to my own. I had a call I needed to make. The sooner the better.

TWENTY-FIVE

EMMA

I felt lighter after leaving the salon and it wasn't because of the trim. Faith had only cut an inch or so off. What had me smiling was her advice which was how I ended up at Queen's Unmentionables.

Olivia's smiling face greeted me when I entered. "How can I help you on this bright morning?"

"Faith sent me by," I said.

Her eyes twinkled with mirth. "She did, did she?"

I nodded. "I'm taking her advice."

"Do you want something for your upcoming honeymoon?" she asked.

Could it possibly be true that she hadn't heard? "Actually, no. The wedding is off."

She arched her eyebrow. "Well, then. Should I guess who the lucky guy is?"

What harm did it cause in telling her? I gave it twenty-four hours before the entire town knew that Aiden and I were together.

"No judgment here," she added.

"Aiden," I said.

Her grin widened. "Good for you. I have the perfect thing," she said, and then I was immersed in the world of seduction, something I didn't know a lot about.

I left with a little black bag, proud of myself. Aiden wanted to wait. I was banking he'd change his mind when he saw me in the little number I'd picked up.

My next stop was the grocery store. I wanted to pick up a bottle of wine and hoped I would run into Alana. To my luck, she was at the register, serving customers. When it was my turn at checkout, I tossed out what I wanted to tell her.

"It's official, I'm seeing your brother."

She rolled her eyes. "Like I didn't see that coming. It's been in the making since high school."

"We didn't date in high school."

"Exactly, but those long lingering gazes were hard to miss. Just don't call me with your relationship drama. I don't want to be in the middle of that." She held up a hand. "And don't tell me about sex with him either. Gross."

I laughed, as I took my wine and teasingly promised to give her all the details anyway. By the time I made it to the bar, I was practically hovering on air. My phone buzzed.

"Hello?" I didn't recognize the number.

"Emma Hawkins?"

"This is she."

"Hi, this is Grady Jackson with Dream BIG travel agency."

"Yeah, hey." I had no idea why he'd be calling me.

"I'm sorry to call you about this. Your father bought tickets for you and Evan."

"Honeymoon," I said to myself.

"Yes."

It was like a lance through my heart. Dad hated Evan,

yet he'd gotten me a thoughtful gift for a wedding that was no longer going to happen. "Can it be canceled?"

"He did buy the trip insurance—"

"But?" I asked.

"But, that insurance relates to you and Evan, not your dad."

"I'm stuck with it?"

"Kind of. I can probably switch Evan's tickets to another name or cancel if we can get credits."

"I'm not marrying Evan. So cancel it."

"Are you sure?"

"Yes, and thank you."

"One more thing," he began. "I run a real estate agency as well if you'd like to sell or buy anything."

"I'll keep that in mind."

Jack called me to the front to help. Apparently, two of our waitresses called out sick. Just as I was ushering the last of our lunch patrons, Darcy walked in and took a seat at the bar.

I forced a smile because I did have to live here. We would run into each other and I didn't want it to be awkward.

"Emma," she said when I returned behind the counter.

"Yes, Darcy."

"I thought we should talk."

I glanced around and there was no one in the area. My bartender had gone on their break.

"Say what you have to say," I said.

"I wanted you to hear it from me. I hooked up with Evan."

I folded my arms. "I guessed. Did you want to rub it in my face?"

"He swore things were over between the two of you."

"Of course, he did. You're welcome to him, or is pain a hard limit for you?" Okay, that had been mean, but it was too late to take back. Apparently, she'd seen the humor.

"Ha. Ha. Ha. He's a psychopath. If I were you, I'd leave town. He's obsessed with you."

"You'd like that wouldn't you?" I asked.

"I would."

"Is that all?" At this point, I wanted her to leave.

She narrowed her eyes in the face of my sarcasm. "Not exactly. Did Aiden tell you I come over once a week and we spend time together, eating pizza."

I lifted my shoulders and let them fall like I didn't have a care in the world. "Aiden doesn't have to check in with me. I trust him."

"Pretend not to care all you want. I'm tired of living in your shadow and I'm not giving up Aiden without a fight," she said.

"I'm not fighting you over a guy. Besides, I would kick your ass. But if you haven't gotten the memo, Aiden chose me."

She got up from her seat and tossed the ring Evan had given me on the counter. She'd taken it. "For now. He'll get bored with you and come back to me. He always does. He never stays away for long. So enjoy yourself while you can."

I will not hate her. I will not hate her, I repeated in my head. I hated her.

DRINKING RUSH WAS WORSE LATER. IT FELT LIKE everyone in town wanted an escape. Down two people, I couldn't leave early. I was stuck until closing time. It was late when I arrived at Aiden's. I used the key he left me. He'd texted me that he'd left it in the same place.

He wasn't downstairs, so I went upstairs. He was on the bed with one arm folded behind his head and his eyes glued to the TV. I dropped my bag in the chair in the corner. Then, I proceeded to remove my clothes.

Once done, I stood in the lacy bodysuit I'd paid good money for at Queen's Unmentionables. His eyes had tracked me the entire time.

"Your hair looks nice," he said, his smile half-cocked.

"That's what you noticed?" I shifted on my feet feeling more confident than I had all my life.

"I notice everything about you when you walk into a room."

"Do you now?" I asked.

"Yes. I'm just waiting for you to come closer."

"Yeah," I said, moving forward.

He snagged my wrist and I giggled as he tumbled me onto the bed.

"I take it, waiting is over," he said.

My answer was ruined by the sound of his phone ringing. He exhaled. "I have to get that."

He was a cop and was never truly off duty especially in a small town like this.

I couldn't hear the other side of the conversation. What I did get was a lot of grunts until he said, "I'm on my way." Then he turned to me. "I'm sorry Emma. I have to go."

He rolled me onto my back and kissed me before jumping out of bed. He rushed to get dressed. It didn't escape my attention when he strapped on a bulletproof vest and a shoulder hostler before leaving.

"Be safe," I said as he left.

Was this what all spouses and partners felt when their significant other left for duty? I talked myself out of worry because we didn't live in LA. This was Mason Creek.

Nothing ever happened here, except my dad. Aiden would be okay. He had to be.

TWENTY-SIX

AIDEN

As MUCH AS I wanted to stay with Emma, Sam had called for backup. He pulled over a vehicle because of a busted taillight. There was something in the hole that made it suspicious outside of the normal repair that needed to be made. He followed procedure and was waiting for back up before he approached.

Based on his account of what was happening, I didn't like the sound of things either. It worried me that Sam was alone on a two-lane road on the outskirts of town. I didn't waste time and put on my issued bulletproof vest and holster before jogging down the stairs. Once I was in my vehicle, I tore down the highway like Sam's life depended on it because it may very well be.

I pulled behind Sam's service vehicle. I radioed over to him that I would approach the vehicle. Because it was after hours, county dispatch was on the line and not Bess.

My hand was on the butt of my weapon as I approached the vehicle Sam had pulled over. I signaled to him to watch my back as I did so, though he was trained to do just that. Wyatt was in route, but he'd been on the other side of town.

The older model sedan engine was still on. As I got closer, I signaled for the driver to roll the window down. The back windows were tinted. That left me at a disadvantage to see if other occupants were in the back. The driver rolled down the window a few inches.

"I'm Chief Deputy Sheriff Faulkner. Do you know why you've been pulled over?"

"No, sir."

It was a good sign that they'd complied so far. But that didn't mean I would take my hand off my weapon.

"You have a busted taillight. Driver's license and registration," I asked for.

"Sure man."

While he was retrieving that, I asked, "Did you know that your taillight was broken?"

"No, sir."

There was too much movement in the car I couldn't see, but I heard.

"There is something sticking out. Can I check your trunk?"

"Why?" he asked.

I didn't have the ability to compel the driver to do so without probable cause that someone's life was in immediate danger. "It's dark. There is something sticking out."

"I don't have to, do I?" He didn't wait for an answer. "So no," he slurred.

He'd given short answers before. His slur had me worried he was driving under the influence. The next minutes would decide the outcome of this traffic stop.

"Please exit the vehicle," I commanded.

Several things happened at once. A muffled cry and pounding could be heard from the back, possibly the trunk, as the driver said, "Aww man. You shouldn't have," to either me or the person trapped.

There was a flash before the sound of a gun discharging. I had my gun out as the punch hit my chest taking me off my feet. I got off a shot before I saw stars as the back of my head hit the pavement.

Chaos ensued. With my vision off, my ears took over. I heard Sam shouting for whoever to get down as sirens approached. I rolled to my side, not wanting to make myself a bigger target as the back door flew open.

I aimed and fired on the person attempting to exit the vehicle with what appeared to be a sawed-off shotgun.

It was over shortly after that. I rolled on my back still trying to catch my breath.

"Aiden, are you okay?" Sam said, crouching next to me.

I nodded. "Did you check the trunk?"

His eyes widened.

"You didn't hear?"

"I'm on it," he said and left.

Though it hurt like a son of gun, I was pretty sure the bullet caught my vest.

"Shit," Sam called.

I forced myself to sit up. "What do you see?"

"A girl," he said.

Wyatt was there with a helping hand. I got to my feet and shuffled over to the trunk. There, bound and gagged, was a young girl. Though I couldn't be sure, I had a feeling she was the missing girl from the BOLO. Her foot was lodged in the left back taillight.

"Call the paramedics," I directed, but not for me.

Wyatt used his radio to inform dispatch as Sam and I helped free the young girl. By the time an ambulance arrived, we had the girl sitting in Sam's squad car with a blanket around her.

I waved off any care for me and directed their attention to our young charge. With no visible injuries, they had no choice but to take my word for it. The last place I wanted to be was the hospital when there was little they could do for me. When the ambulance took her, Wyatt followed. He and Sam wanted me to go to the hospital as well, but I made my excuses.

"I wasn't hit. I'll be fine," I told them.

Reports would be filled, but not tonight. I headed home.

Fearing that Emma was asleep, I did my best to keep quiet as I entered the house. I was working the straps on my bulletproof vest on the deflated sofa when Emma ran down the stairs calling my name until she spotted me.

In an instant, she was by my side with one knee on the sofa to help her balance as she leaned over to help me unclip the straps.

"Are you okay?" she asked. "I heard you'd been shot."

I wasn't sure who she'd heard it from. "I'll be fine once I get this off," I wheezed.

The door burst open, and Darcy came into view. "Of course, the Virgin Mary is here," she announced.

Emma barely glanced her way. "Good thing, someone needed to be here to save him from the devil."

"Ladies," I managed to say as I caught my breath. I wasn't sure if it was the pain or the fact that I couldn't stop staring at Emma's lips.

"Maybe some mouth to mouth might help," Emma said. She winked before closing the last inches of space between us to press her soft lips to mine.

Slow clapping reminded me we weren't alone. "Mediocre performance if you ask me," Darcy said.

"No one's asking you," Emma retorted.

"You're trying to mark your territory. But Aiden was between my thighs before you filled out your training bra. I doubt you got him hard with that kiss. Let me show you how it's done."

It might have been a teenage fantasy of mine to have these two women at the same time, but that was then. I won't lie and say it could be fun in the moment. It would also spell disaster for me in the morning. They would both hate each other and me. Emma hating me wasn't an option.

"Ladies," I said again. Then I met Darcy's gaze. "Darcy, thanks for stopping by. But I'm fine. You can go now."

Her eyes narrowed. "Why am I not surprised you're choosing her," she sneered.

"Darcy," I warned. "You know my feelings. I've been honest with you from the beginning."

She didn't bother with a response and stormed out as quickly as she'd shown up.

Emma finished helping me out of my vest and placed it on the coffee table. She didn't stop there. She helped me out of my shirt, too, and ran her hand over a bruise that had formed. I winced.

"Shouldn't you see a doctor?"

"They aren't going to do anything. I've been hit before with gunfire while wearing a vest. But you can help," I said, slipping a hand to stroke her thigh. "I really like when you're wearing my shirt."

"I was wearing less but didn't want to distract you."

"You could be covered head to toe and I'd be distracted," I admitted.

I tugged her down, ignoring the sharp pain in my chest and kissed her hard. She opened for me and I slid my tongue in her mouth. I might have groaned from pain or the sheer pleasure of kissing her.

"Remember when I said I'm a patient man?" I made sure my eyes were steady on hers when she nodded. "I lied."

My hand found the hem of her shirt and slipped underneath. I took my time skimming up her to the underside of her breast, giving her enough time to put the brakes on things. I sighed when her breast was in my palm, soft yet firm. My mouth watered for more.

She caught my hand and I bit back a curse. It was her right to stop things. She surprised me by her next statement. "Take me to bed, Aiden."

There wouldn't be a need to ask me twice. My ribs hurt something fierce. It would be easier to do it right here on the sofa. But my first time with Emma would be something we'd both remember. So I forced myself up, keeping her in my arms. Praying to heaven above I wouldn't pass out from pain as I carried her up the stairs and into my bedroom.

When I crossed the threshold, I said, "I believe I've waited my entire life for this."

TWENTY-SEVEN
EMMA

Never in my life had a man carried me to bed. Aiden did it effortlessly even when I could tell he was in pain.

"We don't have to," I said. "I know you're hurt."

His smile warmed every part of me. "Being with you will make it better."

We took it slow. I helped him undress and then did a show for him as I removed his shirt I wore until all I had on was my lacy bodysuit. He held out his hand and I took it to be drawn to stand between his legs. He reached up and peeled the straps of the lacy bodysuit down until gravity took over.

There I stood bare in front of him.

"Beautiful," he said.

He cherished me in a way I'd never experienced. He showed every part of me attention before he took me in his arms and rolled me onto the bed.

He went for this kiss and not knocking my legs apart. I'd appreciate his lingering ministrations later, not now when all my nerve endings were ready to fire. I bit his lips and begged for him to move to the good part. "Please."

His mischievous grin turned up a notched as he kissed his way between my breasts to my belly button. When his mouth did delicious things between my thighs, I fisted my hands in his sheets and begged for more.

Aiden didn't disappoint on any level. He lived up to his reputation. By the time he penetrated my depths, I was desperate for him as he filled me. In one thrust, I was ready to blow. Somehow, he took me to another level where stars burst behind my eyes.

True to his word, our lovemaking was slow and built with every moment to a new and higher level. Every slide deeper, I clenched tighter, raising the pleasure once again. He swallowed my moans with soul-searing kisses. He worked the bundle of nerves between my legs until my toes curled and the dam broke. I opened my eyes wanting to look into his as we came together as one.

The man was as beautiful outside as he was in. He didn't end our connection. Just held me tighter to him. I lay there in bliss wondering how I'd ever considered marrying Evan. With him, everything was a rush to the finish.

Though I thought it might be over, Aiden wasn't. It was long into the night, an almost perfect night, before we fell asleep.

Early that morning, Aiden kissed my temple. "Stay asleep."

I was too sleepy to do anything more than murmur something imperceptible before burrowing deeper onto his side of the bed.

Sometime later, I stretched and found the bed empty. It took a few moments of blinking for my vision to clear and remember that Aiden had left earlier.

Downstairs I found coffee and a note.

Keep the key, A

We were really doing this. I wasn't exactly sure on all the rules. Did I need to give him a key to my place? It was probably a good idea that someone had a key since Dad was gone.

That gave me pause. I breathed through the ache that blossomed on my chest. A tear spilled from my eye a second before my phone buzzed. I answered.

"Is this Ms. Hawkins?"

"Yes."

She introduced herself as an employee of the private autopsy firm I'd hired. "I'm calling to let you know that we have the results of your father's autopsy. We can schedule a meeting to go through the results or we can send you the results and schedule a meeting after for any questions you have."

"Please send me the results and then I'll schedule a meeting. Thanks."

She confirmed where I wanted the results emailed before we ended the call.

Though I wanted to speak to Aiden, I knew he was at work. I texted him instead.

Then, I got all cleaned up before leaving his place with the key. I might have squealed a little as I left. Aiden and I were really doing it, and it felt right.

I drove back to my house and sat in the car for a while looking out the window. This house was the dream my father gave my mother. It was also the place where all those dreams died. If I stayed in Mason Creek, I couldn't live in this house. I also couldn't give it up.

It wasn't until I was in the office at the bar that I finally checked my email. The report was there, but fear kept me from opening it. I was afraid to learn he'd been murdered because I just couldn't believe that someone in town would do such a thing. Dad was well liked. Conversely, I feared he wasn't murdered, and I had his grave disturbed for nothing.

My finger hovered over the mouse as I debated what to do. It was almost a relief when one of my employees walked in with a problem. I could walk away for at least a little while before I had to face the results.

Relief filled me when Aiden walked through the door hours later. I didn't care what people thought. I wanted the world to know that I was with this man. I walked over to him and wrapped my arms around him.

"Thank you for coming," I said in his ear.

He put his forehead to mine. "Always."

I angled my head back before pressing my lips to his in a quick kiss. I didn't bother to survey anyone around me. I guided him to the back and into the office. Once seated, I turned the computer in his direction. "I don't think I can look."

There was tenderness in his expression toward me that made me fall a little harder for him as he clicked some keys. I watched his eyes move as he read the information.

After a few minutes, I said, "Well?"

He took in a deep breath before he answered. "Manner of death is listed as homicide."

Air in my lungs became trapped as I didn't know how to feel.

"Cause of death is listed as an acute subdural hematoma."

"What does that mean?" I asked, hoping Dad hadn't suffered.

"I think it's a brain bleed. But we should call. There is a phone number listed."

Aiden brought out his phone and dialed, putting it on speaker.

The medical examiner from the private forensic lab I'd hired answered the phone.

"This is Aiden Faulkner and Emma Hawkins. We are calling about the autopsy results for Doug Hawkins," he said.

"Ah yes. I can schedule a time to go over the results with you in person, but I have a few minutes now."

I found my voice and said, "Can you give a general explanation of your results without all the medical terms."

"I assume that is you, Ms. Hawkins."

"It is."

"I have your permission to discuss this with Mr. Faulkner present?"

"Yes," I said.

"Well, in general terms, it is my medical opinion your father died as a result of a fall on a hard surface which created a hematoma. A hematoma is a brain bleed where the blood is trapped between the skull and the brain tissue. This causes pressure and, in this case, when not relieved causes death."

Aiden spoke. "You listed manner of death as homicide."

"Yes. Under the microscope, I was able to see signs of a leucocyte reaction on the face."

"What's that?" I asked.

"Basically, an early indication of a recent bruise to the face. Such signs can be detected shortly after the impact, which cause it. The bruise would then stop forming after death. My best guess is in layman's terms is that your father was punched which resulted in a hard enough impact with a solid surface to create the brain bleed."

"Did he suffer?" My voice was weak, and I thought I might have to repeat myself.

"In my opinion, no. Based on the size of the bleed, he probably lost consciousness quickly."

Tears spilled from my eyes and I let Aiden take over the conversation.

"This is Aiden again. I'm the chief deputy sheriff stationed in Mason Creek. The initial death certificate states he died of natural causes. Based on your findings, we will open a new investigation. I'll have to have you coordinate with the Coroner's office to make that change."

Jessie's man Miles was the coroner of the county.

"No problem. We do it all the time. We will handle Mr. Hawkins until such time as he can be transferred to the coroner or laid to rest."

"Thank you," Aiden said. "I'll be in touch."

He ended the call and came over. He scooped me out of the seat and then sat with me on his lap. I cried for the hundredth time and figured I'd cry at least a hundred more before I felt even the slightest relief from Dad's loss.

I couldn't tell you how long he held me. At some point, he asked, "Are you going to be okay?" I nodded because I knew he had to get back to work. "I'll see you at home."

Home. He'd said it like it was ours. Choked up, I bobbed my head again and managed a small smile. He sat me back on the chair and placed a lingering kiss on my lips.

"I could stay all night," he said.

"But you need to go and save the world."

"For you."

And just like that, I fell even deeper. I wasn't sure what to call the emotion. But it was far stronger than anything I'd ever felt for Evan.

TWENTY-EIGHT
AIDEN

LEAVING her became harder and harder to do. There was no question about how I felt, and I hoped she understood what I meant when I'd told her I'd see her home. From the moment I'd bought the place, I'd seen her sharing it with me. Some may have considered that cocky. I thought it was determination. My parents always encouraged me to go after what I wanted. I'd wanted Emma for a very long time.

I drove back to the station and sought out the sheriff, who was in his office.

"Do you have a moment?" I asked.

He waved me in, and I waited for his attention to be fully on me before I spoke. "The results are in. The medical examiner from the private autopsy firm Emma hired has ruled Doug Hawkins death as a homicide."

The blood drained from the sheriff's face. "How?"

"Appears he was punched in the face and hit the concrete floor hard enough to cause a brain bleed."

"He didn't have a bruise," Sheriff countered.

"He said the beginning of one could be seen under the microscope."

The next words out of the sheriff's mouth would determine the level of respect I'd have for him going forward.

"The death certificate has to be changed on record by the Coroner's office," he began.

"The coroner is an elected official and doesn't even have to have forensic medical training. The medical examiner has the expertise. I don't think any judge would object to the new findings."

Though our current coroner was a doctor, his expertise was in live patients not dead ones.

He nodded. "We proceed with caution. Until it's changed, legally we can't arrest anyone without damning evidence in hand. Who are you looking at?"

"Jack Riddle, for one."

Shocked registered on his face. "Why?"

"He has motive and opportunity. He claims Doug offered to sell him the bar at some point. What if Doug changed his mind? His will gives everything to Emma with no mention of Jack." The sheriff looked ready to balk, so I dived in. "He had opportunity. He had access to the bar as manager."

"He didn't do it," Sheriff stated.

"Maybe not, but I have to give him a hard look."

"Do you have anyone else?"

"Maybe." I didn't give him more. "I'll need a warrant for that one."

"Get the process moving..." There was a pause and I waited. "And tell Emma I'm sorry."

"You should tell her yourself."

I went to my office to make a boatload of calls. One of those calls was to Jack. An hour later, he showed up to the station voluntarily. I led him back to the small room for interrogations. There was a reason for that.

"What's going on?" Jack asked.

"First, I'm going to read your rights for your protection."

Alarm registered on his face as it did most suspects and witnesses alike who didn't often find themselves dealing with law enforcement. I read him the Miranda warning and offered him a paper with the written warning for him to sign.

"It's procedure," I said, handing him a pen. "I read it because this is being recorded. You're welcome to read it again and then sign, acknowledging you have been made aware of your rights."

He did as I asked, then repeated his earlier question. "What's going on?"

"I'll get to that. First, tell me where you were on the day of Doug Hawkins's death." I gave him the date and window of time I was looking for.

"I was with the guys playing poker until about two."

"Which guys?" I asked and when he named them, I jotted it down. "And after."

"I was at home."

"Was there anyone at home who can corroborate that?"

"My wife."

"Was she sleeping?"

He turned red and I wasn't yet sure if that was embarrassment or anger.

"We were fucking. So yeah. She can corroborate that." So a little of both.

So far, he hadn't asked for a lawyer or questioned my authority. "Do you mind if I give her a call?"

He shrugged, then gestured the go ahead with his hands. He gave me her number and I left the room to place the call. After that ended, I let him go. Even if I'd wanted to, I couldn't arrest him without more.

Though I wasn't in a position to arrest anyone yet, I felt as though things were moving in the right direction by the time I left work that evening. When I got home, I walked into an amazing aroma.

Emma was in the kitchen at the stove wearing another one of my shirts with shorts that barely peeked below the hem. It was sexy as hell. I folded my arms. "Damn, I could come home to this every night."

She turned a lovely shade of pink when she halfway turned to face me. I couldn't resist and placed my hands on her hips while nibbing on her neck. Her giggle only spurred me on.

"If you keep doing that, I'll burn dinner and we'll have nothing to eat."

"Oh, there are a hell of a lot of things to eat that don't involve food."

She swatted at me. "I left work early once Jack returned to make you this meal. You aren't spoiling it for me."

"But I'm hungry for you," I complained with a grin on my face.

"Food first. You're going to need fuel for what I have in mind," she teased. I groaned and she switched topics. "Are you going to tell me why Jack had to leave in the middle of a shift?"

"I have good news and bad news."

She narrowed her eyes but didn't speak.

"Good news is we've opened an official investigation into your father's death." I didn't say murder for good reason. She hadn't said as much, but I could tell part of her wished her father had died of natural causes. That would be easier to swallow than the alternative.

"The bad news?" she asked.

"The bad news is now that things are official, I can't talk about the investigation to anyone, including you."

"Can you at least tell me if Jack is a suspect?" When I sighed, she added, "I need to know if I'm in any danger with him working at the bar. If he killed my dad, he could want me dead too."

She was right. "He has a solid alibi. That's all I can say."

His wife had giving me the same details as he had. Since he hadn't had time to coordinate with her, unless he'd done it beforehand, I had to let him go for now.

"You aren't giving up?" she asked.

"Of course not. I'll find whoever did this. I promise."

She shooed me away after. I assumed she needed a minute, and I went to grab a shower because, like Emma, I had lots of plans for the night.

By the time I dressed in shorts and a T-shirt, Emma had the table set. "Oh, that reminds me," I said. "Will you go to dinner with me at my parents' place on Sunday?" I hadn't been in a while. "I want to make things official."

Her brow lifted. "Official?"

"I hope I can tell them that we're together and that you're moving in." The downright shocked expression on her face made me smile. "It's your fault. You've spoiled me. How can I possible sleep by myself when I know what it's like sleeping with you?"

"Aiden," she said.

"Don't say it's too soon. We've known each other for most of our lives. The little I didn't know about you, we took care of last night."

"But—"

"But, what? I'm only this—" I spread my fingers about an inch apart. "Far away from telling you I'm in love with you."

199

She mimicked my fingers. "Only this much?"

"Yeah, that's only because I don't want to freak you out. And I don't need you to say it. You'll get there."

"Cocky much?"

"My cock can be a bit much at times. But you can take it." I winked.

She laughed and by God I was hard. "You know if I didn't think your ego would blow up like a hot air balloon, I might agree with you. But I guess you'll have to wait and see. Now eat."

"Yes, ma'am."

The food was delicious and rivaled my mother's cooking though I'd never tell Mom. I polished off my plate, sat back, and patted my belly. "A meal like that can put you to sleep," I joked.

She got up and hook her thumbs in those tiny shorts and let them fall. "I think dessert will keep you up."

Then, she ran and, damn right, I chased her because dessert was exactly what I needed. And when I came the first time that night, I couldn't help but imagine Emma pregnant with our child.

TWENTY-NINE

EMMA

AIDEN WAS A CONSIDERATE LOVER. He gave and gave until I was completely satisfied before claiming a release for himself. The man was perfect, and I wondered how I deserved it. Especially, when the next morning, I awoke to the aroma of coffee and baked goods.

He came upstairs and brought them to me.

"You went to town and came back."

"I'll do it every day if you agree to move in with me."

God, the man was beautiful. "Bribing me, are you?"

"Whatever it takes."

"A corrupt officer," I teased.

"As Chief Deputy Sheriff, I plead the fifth. As the man who wants you in his bed, I'll do whatever to keep you here."

"Coffee and pastries are a good start." He sat on the bed looking sexy in his uniform shirt. I rubbed a hand over his chest. "How's the pain?"

He covered my hand. "Insignificant when you're touching me."

I grinned. "I'm serious. I'm worried about you."

"Another reason to move in. Someone to check on me."

"Aiden," I pleaded.

"At least say you'll be here tonight. We can decide day by day and then you can explain to my parents."

I laughed when he fake-pouted. "Alright." His frown turned upside down. "Tonight. I'll be here tonight."

He kissed me then and took the hand he covered and placed it on his hard cock. "See what you do to me. I'm going to be late."

He rolled me onto my back and reminded me of all the reasons he was the best lover I'd ever had.

When he was gone, I called Jessie.

"What? What happened? It's like early. You don't normally get up this early."

"I haven't even gone for a run," I admitted.

"Be still my heart. Is the sky falling?" she teased.

"So... what is everyone saying?" If anyone would have heard, it would be Jessie as her coffee shop is always filled with gossiping townspeople.

"Um, let's see." I imagined her tapping her chin. "There's the one about seeing you and Aiden kissing near the salon. True or False."

I groaned. I hadn't thought anyone had seen. "True."

"And there's the hot kiss at the bar. True?"

"Yes. I didn't care if anyone saw. What else are they saying?" I asked.

"I'm still chuckling over Tate's headline a while back, *Does LAPD stand for Love All People Dutifully or Dearly as a certain Bar Owner claimed or Just Los Angeles Police Department. I think she meant what she said. Love Dearly, just not the 'all' part. A certain chief deputy maybe?* Quick thinking girl, but no one bought that."

I groaned. "You know I don't read the MC Scoop. What else?"

"I don't read it often either. But people talk at the coffee shop. I think Tate's recent headline is *To Kiss or Not To Kiss. That's not the question. But rather if a certain runaway bride is heading to a different groom. Love is in the air* or something like that."

"Say it's not so," I whined.

"Surprisingly yes. But honestly, people seem happy for you and him. I don't think they liked your fiancé much," she laughed.

"He was only in town a few days and didn't talk to many folks."

"Exactly. They thought he was a pompous ass."

"They were right," I said. My dad had been right too. Then I blurted, "Aiden and I hooked up, then he asked me to move in with him."

She choked up for a moment. "Okay. I need to take this step by step. How good was he?"

"Mind blowing?"

"Okay," she said. "Not surprised, considering the rumors. I'm also not completely surprised, he asked you to move in. You two have been headed in this direction since high school."

"You don't think it's too soon?" I asked.

"Too soon for who? How do you feel?"

How did I feel? "I'm scared it won't work out."

"Why? Because you've dated assholes before?"

"Exactly."

"And you've known Aiden how long? Do you think he's an asshole, really?"

"No. But he didn't exactly have the best reputation when it came to girls in school."

"What hot boy in town did when girls threw themselves at them?" she asked.

"Girls like Darcy?"

"Exactly like her. She pinned that boy down to the point of pain."

"Pain?" I asked.

"Yeah, like painful to watch when everyone knew he wanted you."

I burst out laughing. "Would it be weird if I thought I was in love with him?" I asked.

"Um... Let me think. You've known him how long again? We covered that right. And his parents too. It's not like he's some random dude you met on the street. I'd be shocked if you weren't in love with him already. The boy had mad puppy dog eyes when he came in this morning wanting to get you coffee."

"That was sweet."

"Sweet. He's damn near perfect."

"You never said this about Evan."

"Evan was an asshole. I supported you because that's what best friends are for," she said. "Anyway, I've got to go. The line is getting long. Tell Aiden you'll move in with him and say the L word too."

She hung up before I could comment. I thought about what I could do to make the night perfect.

I went to work early to do the books, check inventory, and place orders. I left after the lunch rush. Jack had been cleared of any wrongdoing, so I would let him do the job my father had given him.

At home, when I walked in, I felt different. I'd come to the decision that I couldn't live here with all the memories. I also couldn't give it up. I texted Aiden to come by after work as I went to my room and surveyed it. My room hadn't changed much over the years except for what hung on the walls. Posters were gone, but the furniture was the same. I made a plan and went to work.

When Aiden arrived, dinner was ready. I marveled how easy it was to be with him. He walked in and greeted me with a kiss. It all felt so natural.

"You're spoiling me," he teased.

"I actually like cooking." Which was true. "Dad and I would cook together."

"We could do that."

I granted him a big smile. "We could."

As we ate, I said, "There is a reason why I asked you here."

His brow arched.

I took a deep breath before speaking. "I wanted you to share with me my last meal in this house."

"Are you saying what I think you're saying?"

I did my best to hold it together because it still was home. It always would be. "Before you asked, I'd already decided to move. It's hard to be here without my parents."

"You're selling?"

I shook my head. "I can't do that either. I thought about maybe turning it into a bed and breakfast. I think my parents would approve. It's not like we have lodging in town."

He looked impressed. "Wow. That sounds like a great idea."

"I thought so. Plus, it will be something I did. A business I created on my own."

"I like. You would have to get approval by the town council."

"Yeah, but it's a win. I'm creating jobs. And I'm only

renting out the three rooms upstairs. I don't expect a lot of foot traffic."

"I think it's a great idea."

I smiled because I loved his unconditional support. "There is something else."

"What's that?" he asked as he took another bite of his food.

"I needed someone here with me as I go through Dad's stuff. He wouldn't want his things to go to waste."

He took my hand in his and threaded our fingers. "I can be with you every step of the way."

THIRTY

AIDEN

It was hard leaving Emma in the morning after an emotional night. We didn't get through everything. Her father hadn't had an excess of clothes, but as we pulled them out, some brought memories back for her. I reminded her that it wasn't a race and that she had time. She didn't have to get rid of everything.

She'd packed some of her things and brought them over to my place. She was surprised I'd already made space for her in what was now our room.

Over the next few days, we found a rhythm. I'd bring her breakfast and she made us dinner. It was so easy I wondered why I'd waited so long.

The change in her father's death certificate went rather smoothly. I'd been able to obtain the signed warrant I needed that morning and had just submitted it to the rental company electronically when Bess said I had a visitor. I asked her to send him in.

I stood when he walked in. "How can I help you?" I asked.

He handed me a card. Before I could look at it, he introduced himself as an insurance investigator. "We were in the process of working through a claim when I was notified the manner of death of Mr. Doug Hawkins was changed to homicide."

"Only now?"

"We have up to sixty days to pay out a policy."

"How can I help?"

"I'm investigating the beneficiary. He checked his phone. A Ms. Emma Hawkins. We won't pay out a policy to anyone related to the murderer and including the murderer."

"What are you saying? Do you think Emma had something to do with her father's death?"

"I'd say he'd taken out a two-million-dollar policy only a few weeks before his death."

That surprised me with the timing. In no way did I believe Emma was capable or responsible for her father's death, but I had to ask the question if only to poke holes in his theory. "Did Emma file a claim?"

He paused. "Actually yes. She did on a smaller policy that Mr. Hawkins had for quite some time."

"Then, why are you here, in person?"

"It's a large policy and the timing."

"But you just said she didn't file a claim."

"She didn't. But once the other policy was triggered, it was linked to the larger policy."

"Did you pay out the smaller policy?" I asked.

"We did."

"So, you didn't do an investigation on that one?"

"That policy was paid in full, and it wasn't immediately linked to the larger policy until after the smaller one was paid out. If she were to be found guilty, we would of course try to recover the payment on the smaller policy."

I wanted to burst the bubble of the smug bastard. "I can tell you this much because it's not a part of our current investigation, but Emma was the one that pushed to say her father was murdered. She said that from the beginning. She paid for the private autopsy that ultimately opened a murder investigation."

He wasn't moved. "If you won't investigate her, I will."

I wanted to punch the smug bastard, but I remained calm. Sheriff popped his head in. I wasn't sure how much he heard. "Of course, we will investigate Ms. Hawkins as procedure dictates. In fact, I'll be interviewing her this afternoon. I'll be sure to have Aiden pass on our findings."

The man stood and held out his hand. I didn't take it. The sheriff did. They exchanged introductions before the guy left.

"Emma didn't do this," I protested once I knew the insurance investigator was out of earshot.

"Maybe not, but you should know any good defense attorney will question why we didn't. So we do." He held up a hand to stop me so he could finish. "You're too close to her. Another weapon a defense attorney could use. So I'll do it."

He was right. "Fine, but I'm watching."

"As long as you keep your cool. I can't go soft on her Aiden. You know this."

I did. That didn't mean I had to like it. Still, I had to wonder why Emma's father took out such a large policy. Was he in fear of his life?

Gaining access to his email and phone would be as easy as calling Emma. But again, I had to follow procedure so anything that I found could be admitted into evidence. Up until this point, I'd made the mistake of thinking this case was simple. Now it was time to find out what Doug was doing leading up to his death.

My finger hovered over my phone. I couldn't call Emma and warn her. I just hope she understood when I explained later, why I couldn't. My cell phone records could be subpoenaed in the future. They could tie a call from me to her before Sheriff interviewed her. It would look bad and give the real killer reasonable doubt in jurors' minds. So I put down my phone and prayed she'd forgive me.

I'd been listening for Emma showing up since the sheriff didn't tell me when she was due to arrive. I also didn't ask. When I heard her up front, I left my office and went directly to the viewing room with the one-way glass to see into the interrogation room. I wasn't hiding. It was better Emma didn't see or hear from me until after the sheriff talked to her.

A camera was set up already in the room. I clenched my fist as the sheriff explained he would be turning it on and then read her the Miranda warning. She shouldn't be here, I thought.

The sheriff laid into her. "Emma, can you tell me where you were the night of your father's death?"

"In bed. Why are you asking me this? You asked me these things after you found him."

"This is for the official record now that we have proof he was murdered."

I could see the anger in her face as she figured out why she was there. "Proof I paid to get. I told you from the beginning I thought Dad was killed."

"I know that, Emma. But I have to ask. Please tell me where you were that night."

"In bed. Alone and no, no one was with me."

"Not even Evan?" Sheriff asked.

"No. Dad wouldn't allow us to share a room because we weren't married."

"Where did Evan sleep?"

"In the downstairs room."

"Would you know if he left the house?" he asked.

"No."

"Would he know if you left the house?"

She shrugged. "It's possible. The room is in the back, but if the house was silent, I suppose he might hear the front door open."

"But you couldn't?"

"I had ear buds in that night."

"Is that something you normally do?"

"Sometimes," she said.

"But that night you did?"

"Yes," she said.

"Do you know your father's state of mind that night?"

I scrubbed a hand over my face because this was a damning piece of evidence that could be used against her.

"The last I saw him, he wasn't happy. He and Evan didn't get along and things turned ugly at the dinner table."

"What was said?" Sheriff asked.

"Evan asked my father about his no sleeping in the same room rule. Dad said he didn't have to explain himself. It was his house. Evan told Dad he was too old fashion and that he and I had slept together many times so saving my virtue was far too late." I hoped the next time I met Evan we weren't in Mason Creek and I wasn't on duty. "Dad told him he didn't deserve any of my virtue and he hoped I'd wake up before I made the biggest mistake of my life."

"What happened next?"

"I told them to stop. I told Dad no one was ever good enough for me in his eyes. I told Evan that he should leave in the morning if he couldn't respect my father. Then, I left."

"Did you see your father after that?" Sheriff asked.

She shook her head but finally answered no.

"What about Evan?"

"He came up to my room and I told him to leave."

"He came upstairs even though your father was home."

"Yes, and it pissed me off. I knew then things were finished with us."

That I hadn't know.

"Did you tell Evan things were over?"

"No. I just wanted him to leave. I thought about going to talk to Dad but decided to wait until morning and it was too late." Her words ended in a muffled sob.

"Just a few more questions, Emma. Did you leave your room at any time that night and notice if your father or Evan were gone?"

"No. I woke up just before you came to the door and Evan came out of his room."

"Was that the first time you saw Evan that morning?"

"Yes," she answered.

"You said you couldn't hear if someone left, right?"

"That was with my ear buds in. I took them off at some point in the night. Your banging was quite incessant." She sniffled and I wanted to bring her tissues.

"Did your father have an insurance policy?"

She nodded. "He had a small twenty-five-thousand-dollar policy. I used it to pay for his funeral and pay off his truck."

"So, you are unaware of any other policy he might have had?"

"He didn't have any other one," she said.

"Did he mention considering buying a policy?"

"No."

"If I told you your father took out a two-million-dollar policy a month or two before he died, you would be surprised?"

She nodded. "I would."

"Okay, that's all Emma." Sheriff got up and turned off the recording.

"That's all. You brought me here to accuse me of murdering my father for insurance money?" she shouted. "He didn't have any other policies. I checked through his things."

"No. I did this to protect you because as I'm sure you will learn, he did take out a policy."

"No," she whispered.

"Yes."

She looked in disbelief. "Please don't tell anyone. I don't want anyone looking at me differently."

"This is a part of an investigation." He looked at the mirror when he said it. "None of it can be spoken about until the trial. I promise, and if it doesn't come up then, your secret is safe with me."

The sheriff left the room with the door open. Emma didn't leave. I had a feeling she knew I was on the other side of the glass.

THIRTY-ONE

EMMA

It didn't take long for Aiden to walk into the room. As I suspected he'd been behind the glass.

"Did you know that was going to happen?" I asked. There was a knife's edge to my tone I couldn't take back.

He held up his hands in a pleading gesture as he said, "Yes."

"You couldn't warn me, could you?" I'd seen enough cop shows to figure it out.

"No."

His eyes pleaded me to understand. "You couldn't contact me because of our relationship, and it could be used against both of us."

He nodded.

"Do you think I had anything to do with it or this money?" I spat.

"Hell no," he said and closed the distance. "Of course, I didn't. But he had to do it for the record. We couldn't leave holes a defense team could use in their favor."

"Why would Dad take out a policy?"

"I have the same question. Do you have any ideas?"

"None."

"Do you know if your father used an insurance agent or just bought insurance online?"

"I think he had an agent. He has policies to cover the bar for theft, fire and other business insurances."

"Can you get me the name of your agent?"

"I thought you couldn't talk to me about the case."

"I'm not. I'm gathering information. I would ask that you don't contact the agent. If they contact you, that's fine. At least until after I speak to them and get the information I need."

"Okay," I said. "Can I ask if you're any closer to solving this case?"

"I have a theory," he said.

"But you can't tell me."

He silently agreed before kissing my forehead. "Will you be home tonight?"

Alarm filled me. "Are you kicking me out?"

"No. I just—"

"Aiden, today sucked. But I don't blame you. I wish we weren't in this situation."

"Me too."

"I might be late since Jack had to come earlier to cover me. I'll probably stay until close."

He feigned a dagger to his heart. "I guess it's hot dogs for me tonight."

I laughed and it felt good after all the anger. "You'll survive."

"Maybe, maybe not. You've spoiled me." He kissed me lightly. "Get back to work."

And I did. I returned home late at night; Aiden was up in his room watching TV. He turned it off when I came in. "Hey stranger, I thought you'd never get home."

"Missed me?" I teased, enjoying our banter.

"Missed you, I'm not whole until you're with me."

I spun around and my jaw opened. "Mr. Faulkner, did you steal that line from somewhere?"

"No. But you stole my heart."

I moved over and crawled on the bed. He caught me and rolled us on our sides. "You've got all the lines tonight."

"I'm just not holding back anymore. You have to understand, you're it for me. My father told me that when I found my person, I'd know it. You are my person, Emma."

There was no holding back now. "I'm falling in love with you Aiden. So no jokes, okay?"

"No jokes. I'm serious about this, about you, about us." I was caught in the web of his gaze. "That's why I need you to do one thing for me."

"What's that?"

"Don't be alone tomorrow."

AIDEN

I COULDN'T ANSWER HER QUESTIONS SO I FILLED THE spaces where words would have been with tender kisses and soft touches until she burned with desire. Then I filled her other places until she begged for release. I'd learned her rhythm and the tempo she needed to cross into bliss. I gave her everything she needed to get there. I held her tight because I knew what was coming, and I hated it for her.

Tomorrow was that day. All the pieces had come together. It was time to topple the bastard that had caused harm to Emma's father and left her with the pain of it.

There was no perfect murder. Everyone made mistakes. You just had to find them.

I'd made a request to interview a person of interest and it was agreed to. I had my questions lined up in my head, but I also had notes and pictures ready to use.

When the bastard arrived, I had Bess escort the person of interest and their lawyer to the integration room. I left them there long enough to make the killer sweat.

I walked in and dropped my folder on the table between us. The sound broke the silence for a second. The lawyer and his client turned in my direction. They'd been quietly conversing.

"First, I'm going to let you know this is being recorded." I gestured toward the camera before walking over and turning it on. "Now, I'll read you your rights." I recited the Miranda warning remembering the look on Emma's face when it had been said to her because of this asshole.

I finally sat, placing the Miranda warning statement on the table. "Please sign." I slid the page halfway over and the lawyer took it. He scanned the page before giving his client the okay to sign.

"Mr. Evan Daily. That is your name, isn't it?" I asked.

"You know it is, asshole," he said before his lawyer could stop him.

I leaned back because I had this one in the bag. "Why don't you tell me where you were the night of Doug Hawkins' death." I gave him the exact date. "Let's say anytime from midnight onward. Oh, and in case you don't know Doug Hawkins is Emma Hawkins, your former fiancée's father."

He glared at me.

"Would you like me to help you with that?"

The lawyer cut in. "Why is my client here?"

"He's a person of interest." The next I said while tapping the table with my index finger. "He's *the* person of interest." When he didn't answer, I pulled out a picture of a rental car and slid it around so they could see. "Does this car look familiar?"

The image had been blown up from a surveillance video shot. The quality wasn't great. Though the timestamp and license plate were clearly read.

"It could be any sedan."

I nodded. "It could be. But do you recall renting a vehicle?"

The reason I hadn't initially come to this conclusion was because I'd assumed Evan had driven his own vehicle to Mason Creek. He had gone to college in Montana. As he and his lawyer decided what to say, I pulled out another document.

"Does this refresh your memory?" I let them see a copy of the rental agreement.

His lawyer gave him the go ahead to speak. "Yeah, I guess I rented the vehicle. I don't remember if it's this specific one."

"The license plate listed on the rental agreement matches the one in the picture, correct?"

He took the time to check both before saying, "Yes."

"As you can see from the timestamp, you were out that early morning on the day Doug died."

"There's no law against that," he said.

"And where were you going? And don't lie. I have video

footage in town." During an interrogation, I could lie all I wanted to. He couldn't.

"I was out for a drive."

"Are you familiar with Darcy Williams?"

His lawyer once again gave him the go ahead. "Yeah, I knew her. I wasn't married."

"So you admit you went to see Darcy a little after midnight?" I asked.

"Yeah, so what? I screwed her."

"Yet, you concealed that fact from Emma. So much so, you parked in the town square and walked the rest of the way to Darcy's apartment."

"And?"

"Why did you drive so slowly past the bar?"

He shrugged. "I was going to park there."

"Why didn't you?"

"There was a car in the lot."

"Whose car?" I asked.

"Doug's," he spit out.

"Let's move forward. You went to Darcy's, had sex, then what?"

"I left."

"Did you encounter anyone after you left Darcy's? And let me caution you, you're under oath. Lying to me is a criminal offense."

He whispered something to his lawyer who nodded.

"I plead the fifth," he said with a sardonic smile on his face.

"Okay. I have video footage of Doug picking you up. Can you tell me why?" I didn't have the pickup portion, but he didn't know that. Sam was canvasing town for more external surveillance videos on buildings around town.

The dumbass was so smug, he blurted, "The sanctimonious bastard was probably going to see Darcy or some other chick but had so much to say about what I was up to," while the lawyer tried to stop him. But Evan only had eyes for me. "I guess that makes us even. We've slept with the same women. Do you have a preference? I know I do."

"For the record, I hadn't been to town to live in years when you were there. I arrived the day of Doug's funeral."

"Yeah, and you couldn't wait to get my fiancée."

I clamped my lips shut because he wouldn't dictate this interrogation. "So Doug took you back to the bar. Why?"

"Don't answer," the lawyer pleaded, but it was as if he hadn't heard him.

"Because he didn't want to shame me in front of Emma."

"This interview is over!" the lawyer demanded. "We're leaving."

"You can't," I said.

"Why not?" the lawyer snapped.

I flashed him a smug grin. "Because your client is under arrest."

Evan leaned forward and slammed his fist on the table. "For what? Punching the old man? He deserved it. He had his back to me while he told me all the reasons I wasn't right for his precious daughter. When he turned around, I reacted."

The lawyer tried to yank him back so they could confer. He didn't let him.

"So you watched him die. I have the footage from inside the bar." Another lie.

Evan sneered at me. "You can't. I took it as proof he was alive when I left. The man tripped over his feet, feel and bumped his head." His lawyer kept telling him to shut up, but he was solely focused on me. "I know my rights. There is no duty to rescue in Montana. You can't arrest me because I didn't call 911. He was breathing. For all I knew, he'd get up in a few minutes. And if he didn't, Emma would be better off. Because of me, the old man bought a new life insurance policy."

That was a shock, and I did my best not to show it. Though I wanted to know why, I continued to goad him into hanging himself. "Yet you took the surveillance video to conceal you'd been with him."

"I took it for my protection." He held up a hand to his lawyer. "I've got this," he said to him.

Since he was distracted, I asked, "Where is it now?"

"The original is in my apartment. I have another on the cloud. I can pull it up on my phone."

"Your apartment in Montana?"

"No, Chicago. I'm done with Montana. I have all the credits I need to graduate with my MBA." He said it like I should be impressed.

"Well, you're going to miss graduation."

He stood but still leaned on the desk like I should fear him. "Fuck you. You have nothing on me."

"Would you like to tell your client, or should I?" The lawyer knew they were screwed. "You see, you admitted to aggravated assault of Mr. Hawkins which is a felony. If your felony results in a death, that's called deliberate homicide here in Montana. You'll be subject to the death penalty. I hope it was worth it. You should have called 911."

Evan lost it and charged at me. I had the benefit of time as he skirted around the table. I let him hit me because that was an assault of a law enforcement officer. Just another assault charge added to the many.

Wyatt and Sam, who'd been watching, came rushing in

and subdued him. We already had county transport ready to take him to a county jail. He was spitting mad.

I turned to his lawyer. "You should know, we have a duly executed search warrant for his apartment in Chicago. Well, the Feds do. I called in a favor to a buddy of mine. Anyway, he's being moved to county."

The lawyer said nothing and walked out.

Though I had paperwork to do, I had to do something first.

EMMA

I HAPPENED TO BE OUT FRONT WHEN AIDEN WALKED into the bar. I smiled before I noticed he wasn't. "What's wrong?"

He glanced around. "Can we talk outside?"

That was unusual. I felt nervous butterflies and not the good kind. My stomach continued to churn as he took my hand and led me out the front door. "You're scaring me," I admitted.

"Let's walk around back."

That freaked me out more. He didn't want anyone to see or hear what he was about to tell me.

At the back of the bar, there was an outdoor area that had a platform deck. We used that for evening summer-time concerts and special barbecue events when we screened sports games. At the moment, it was empty.

He never let go of my hand and we were standing close,

so he didn't have to speak loudly. "We have your father's killer in custody." Alarm filled me. "I wanted you to hear it from me before the rumor mill got started."

"Who is it?" I prayed it wasn't Jack. We'd come so far in our relationship. I didn't want to think he'd betrayed my father that way.

"I don't want you to think this is your fault in any way."

I tried to pull away as anger wanted to take hold. "Just tell me."

"Evan, Emma. Evan punched your father, he fell, and you know the rest. For the record, I don't believe he intended on killing him."

I covered my mouth because I was going to scream as my knees buckled. Aiden caught me. Tears burst from my eyes. "He punched Dad and left him there to die?" I choked up. This was my fault. I brought Evan to see my dad.

"Yes. But I don't think he waited around to see how serious it was. I'm not trying to give him an excuse. I just don't think he's a cold-blooded murderer. He will face the death penalty though."

Nothing Aiden said in that moment penetrated. "It is my fault," I cried.

I don't know how long he held me or how I ended up at his home in bed. He stayed with me the entire time.

There were no words that generated for a long time after. I went through the grief cycle several times before I was coherent.

Hours later, when my tears had dried, I said, "I couldn't have done this without you," as I laid on Aiden's chest, staring into space.

"You made sure your dad got the justice he deserved. I'm just happy I was here to help."

"I thought I wanted to leave this town. I was so

desperate to go, I let myself believe I was in love with the wrong man and Dad paid the price."

"Emma. None of this is your fault. None of it. Evan made a choice. The wrong one. You didn't know what could happen, would happen. And I will always be here for you. My parents will be here for you. They love you as much as I do."

My heart raced with joy I needed to get me through. "It's because of him, I know exactly what love isn't. It's because of you, I know exactly what love is. I love you, Aiden. I don't care if people think it's too soon."

He entwined our fingers together. "I thought it was almost too late. When I came back, I was sure I had lost you for good. You're going to marry me one day, Emma Hawkins. You can count on it."

EPILOGUE

Weeks later

Coming to terms with the circumstance of my father's death may never happen. Somewhere in the weeks that followed, Aiden had almost finished the house. He'd gotten help from Wyatt to replace old floorboards and other carpentry work. Sadie's dad, Burt, who owned Plumbing Solutions, updated the plumbing. Aiden contracted other people in town with work he couldn't do himself. However, I had a feeling he'd find projects to work on around the house.

I graduated from college with my business degree around the same time. Aiden, his parents, and my friends were there for support at the ceremony. It was such as good feeling to have them be there.

Meanwhile, Evan had his initial court hearing, and he wasn't granted bail because the prosecutor claimed he was a flight risk. Though his lawyer was appealing that. I wasn't sure how I felt about Evan facing the death penalty. What he'd done was morally wrong, but I could now agree with Aiden that his intent probably wasn't murder after seeing the video footage inside the bar. He deserved time for sure. But I wasn't a lawyer and would let the legal people worry about that.

I was doing my best to move past all the hurt and pain. Though I didn't want to, I had to release my anger to move forward. It was a day-by-day thing. And tonight was a beautiful evening. The sun was low in the sky as Aiden and I sat in a clearing near the lake. He picked up dinner from the Italian restaurant in town and took me on picnic date.

"What do you think?" he asked, taking another bite of his pasta.

He hadn't worn any hat tonight, and I brushed away a strand of hair covering his eye. "Good. I could have cooked for you," I said.

"Tonight, I wanted you to just enjoy the evening."

I smiled because I'd gotten lucky. I'd dodged a bullet and now I was with a man I adored and who adored me.

"I got the estimates back," I said, enthusiastically. "Work can begin this week."

The life insurance money had come through. I'd opened an account out of town because I really didn't want anyone to know I was technically a millionaire. It didn't feel right to profit from my father's death either.

"He would be happy," Aiden said. "You heard what Evan said."

In interviews with the prosecution, Evan admitted during the argument with my father before he died, Dad had told Evan he'd taken his advice from a phone call they had prior to meeting and had gotten better life insurance so that I wouldn't need Evan in the event of his death. Evan hadn't wanted to be charged with killing my father to get access to the money I would get. Apparently, his family had cut him off. That had been the real reason behind the fake ring. Though his parents paid for his lawyer. They didn't want their name tarnished.

"I know. But I'd rather have my father than the money," I said. He squeezed my hand as I fought tears. "I'm not going to cry."

"You can cry whenever you want. I'll be here."

I wiped my eyes as I nodded. "It's a nice night. Let's talk about something else."

He changed the subject as I asked. "A friend of mine asked me for a favor."

"Should I be worried?"

"It could be a good thing. There are two women who need to relocate. A mother and daughter. I thought maybe the mother would be a good fit to run your bed and breakfast unless you have someone else in mind."

"I don't. But if they're in trouble..."

"Oh, they're good people. The daughter is a registered nurse. I'm going to ask Miles if he needs a nurse in his office. Otherwise, I'm sure she would be willing to help at the B&B."

"I trust you. If you trust this friend and them, we could do that."

His smile warmed my insides and my mind drifted to the moment we'd get home. I was ready for him to show me all the ways he could love me.

"I also hear that Blake Walker and Jack Torres are coming back to town," he said.

"Really? Maybe we should throw them a welcome home party at the bar?"

"You have the kindest heart. I think that's a good thing. We should let them know they're our heroes."

My head spun with ideas. I'd see if the mayor wanted to get involved if they didn't have anything else planned.

When we finished eating, Aiden took my hand and led me into the trees.

"Where are we going?" I asked. "I was hoping to go home." I winked at him.

"Walk with me," he said. "I'll make up for it later."

I bit my lip because I knew he would. "Where are you taking me?" I asked as we were crossing into private property.

He just smiled. Not long after we reached the creek where the most beautiful bridge stood. A man named Henry Davis had built it for his then girlfriend, now wife. Lore had it, he built it to propose to her on it. My heart galloped like wild horses.

I followed him onto the bridge treading lightly. He stopped us at the middle.

AIDEN

IT FELT LIKE I'D WAITED A LIFETIME FOR THIS moment. Though I could see that she understood why I'd brought her here, I had no idea about what I was going to say next.

"Do you remember when I told you that I got some advice once?"

She bobbed her head.

"Your dad gave me that advice."

As her eyes widened, I thought back to that day.

"AIDEN," MR. HAWKINS SAID WHEN I WALKED INTO THE bar. "Back from school?"

I'd gotten back into town earlier that day from college and my first thought was to come here. "Yes, sir."

"You're still not old enough to drink." He eyed me suspiciously.

Emma walked into view and she'd only gotten prettier since the last time I'd seen her. She hadn't looked in my direction, so I got my fill.

"You're here for Emma, are you?"

I snapped my head back in his direction. I wasn't sure what to say. Emma's dad was famous for busting the balls of any guy he didn't think deserved any of her attention. "Yes, sir," I admitted because it was better than lying.

He nodded. "Well, at least your eyes weren't on her ass," he muttered.

I shook my head, nerves getting the better of me. "No, sir."

"Joe and Mary raised a good boy. You have my permission to ask her out."

I'd heard she wasn't dating which was why I came. Every time I'd wanted to ask her out in the past, she had a boyfriend, or I had a girlfriend.

"However," he began. "Let me give you some advice."

"Yes, sir."

"You're going back to college when summer is over, right?"

I agreed.

"*I like you. When I saw you looking at my daughter, it reminded me of how I looked at my wife. I want the man that marries my daughter to love her the way I loved her mother.*"

"*Uhhh.*"

He grinned. "*What I'm saying, Aiden, is do you want a summer with my daughter or maybe a lifetime? If you date her over the summer, it will end when you go back to school.*"

"*Sir—*"

"*You will be far apart and we both know that there will be temptations at school. If you break her heart now, you may not get a second chance.*"

I got what he was saying. Even though I'd broken things off with Darcy before my freshman year thinking I was doing the right thing, she'd still been upset.

"*You need to decide if you want Emma's heart for a summer or for lifetime.*"

When I finished recounting the past, I blinked away the memory and saw Emma crying. Since I thought they were happy tears, I knelt before her, pulling out the box with the ring I'd gotten a few weeks ago from Ryder's jewelry store.

"I know how important it would be for you to have your Dad's approval. I hope maybe that's what he gave me." I took a breath. "I'm asking, will you give me a lifetime and do me the honor of being my wife?"

Emma

. . .

I WASN'T SURE I COULD SPEAK, BUT THERE WAS SO much I had to say. I tugged him to his feet and his expression showed signs of alarm. I smiled. "I need to tell you some things before I answer, and I didn't want you kneeling there that long."

His frown flipped and he graced me with a beautiful smile.

"Thank you for sharing that memory about my dad. It does help, but I would have said yes anyway. But now it makes sense what Dad told me." His brow rose in question. "When I told him I was engaged to Evan, his immediate response was *I thought you were going to marry that Faulkner boy you had a crush on.*"

Aiden's grin widened.

"He shocked me with that. I just assumed he was saying that because he'd figured out that I did in fact have a crush on you. Then, I told him even if I wanted to, you were living in LA and wouldn't be back. He said that you'd be back. And here you are."

His thumb came up and swiped a tear away. "Here I am."

"There's something else you need to know. I was planning to tell you later after all the fun stuff," I paused. "I'm—um—I'm pregnant."

His eyes grew the size of saucers and I waited on bated breath for his reaction because we hadn't talked about starting a family. I didn't know if he wanted kids.

"Emma." He reached down and placed his hands on either side of my belly. "You're carrying our child."

I nodded and murmured an assent. "Are you okay with that?" I babbled.

"Of course. Now you have to marry me."

"That's all I needed to hear. Yes, Aiden, I'll marry you."

What had started off as a beautiful evening was capped off as the perfect night. Aiden did all kinds of crazy and wonderful things to me when we got home. Our home.

I'd like to thank you for taking the time to read my novel. Above all, I hope you loved it. If you did, I would love it if you could spare just a few minutes to leave a review ∼ just a few words are fine. I would greatly appreciate it. Thanks so much!

Though this is the end, there are more books in this world. Read on to find out what stories and how you can get two books from me for FREE.

Did that ending leave you with questions about Liam?

Grab's Liam's story, King Me — HERE.

Aiden's best friend Nate is up next. Grab Perfect Bastard HERE. And grab a free short story with Adien, Emma and Nate. Perfect Holiday (see below)

Love Small Town Romances
Check out others of mine.

Tempting the HeartBreaker - curvy woman + hot rancher. Yum!

MARRIED IN VEGAS - Best Friend's Brother romance

FREE STORIES if you join my newsletter

Perfect Holiday & Honey

ACKNOWLEDGMENTS

A special thank you for the Mason Creek series readers. You guys totally rock.

Special Thank You to our fearless leader C.A. Harms for organizing. And thanks to Lydia and Megan at HEA Book Tours for organizing our releases.

Thanks to Sarah Paige @ The Book Cover Boutique, who made this gorgeous cover for me and the series.

Thanks to Lindee Robinson for the awesome picture for the cover.

To Kate & Kelly at Joy editing— Thanks for all your comments, change suggestions and feedback.

A special thanks to a group of authors who helped me get through a writing slump due to COVID fatigue. No I didn't have COVID, but I couldn't read or write a thing for the longest time. Thanks Jana for organizing the writing zoom group. It's because of Jana along with LIV and Anne that I was able to finish not one but two books in record time. And I'm still going strong.

ABOUT THE AUTHOR

Terri E. Laine, USA Today bestselling author, left a lucrative career as a CPA to pursue her love for writing. Outside of her roles as a wife and mother of three, she's always been a dreamer and as such became an avid reader at a young age.

Many years later, she got a crazy idea to write a novel and set out to try to publish it. With over a dozen titles published under various pen names, the rest is history. Her journey has been a blessing, and a dream realized. She looks forward to many more memories to come.

STALK ME AT

Website: terrielaine.com
Facebook: terrielainebooks
Facebook Page: TerriELaineAuthor
TikTok - @terrielaineauthor
Instagram @terrielaineauthor
Goodreads: terri e laine
Twitter: @TerriLaineBooks
Newsletter Signup:
https://www.subscribepage.com/terrielaine

Join my fan group
Terri's Butterflies or Terri's Bad Girls Group on Facebook.

I have several upcoming releases, make sure to sign up for my newsletter or check my website for details.
www.terrielaine.com

ALSO BY TERRI E. LAINE

Mason Creek

Perfect Night

Perfect Bastard

Perfect Attraction

Mountainside

Resisting Mr. Fancy Pants

Tempting Mr. Heartbreaker

Married in Vegas standalone series

Married in Vegas: In His Arms

Absolutely Mine

King Maker Trilogy

Money Man

Queen of Men

King Maker

Kingdom Come Duet

Kingdom Come

Kingdom Fall

King Me Duet

King Me

Queen Her

All the Kings Sons Standalone Spinoffs

Arrogant Savior

Rook to Ruin

Bishop to King

Pawn to Knight

Him standalone series

Because Of Him

Captivated by Him

Chasing Butterflies standalone series

Chasing Butterflies

Catching Fireflies

Changing Hearts

Craving Dragonflies

Songs for Cricket

Other standalone books

Ride or Die

Thirty-Five and Single

Crown of Thorns

other books co-authored

by Terri E. Laine

Cruel and Beautiful

A Mess of A Man

One Wrong Choice

A Beautiful Sin

Sidelined

Fastball

Hooked

Worth Every Risk

A Beautiful Sin

Dirty Savage Boss

Dirty Arrogant Boss

Made in United States
North Haven, CT
06 May 2023

36317308R00150